GUI

NANCY DREW

girl detective ®

The Old Fashioned Mystery of the Haunted Dollhouse

STEFAN PETRUCHA • Writer
SHO MURASE • Artist
with 3D CG elements by RACHEL ITO
Based on the series by
CAROLYN KEENE

New York

Visit us at www.abdopub.com

Library bound edition © 2006

Spotlight, a division of ABDO Publishing Company Inc., is the
school and library distributor of the Papercutz books.

Library of Congress Cataloging-In-Publication Data

The Haunted Dollhouse
STEFAN PETRUCHA – Writer
SHO MURASE – Artist
with 3D CG elements by RACHEL ITO
BRYAN SENKA – Letterer
CARLOS JOSE GUZMAN
SHO MURASE
Colorists
JIM SALICRUP
Editor-in-Chief

ISBN 10: 1-59707-008-4 paperback edition
ISBN 13: 978-1-59707-008-9 paperback edition
ISBN 10: 1-59707-009-2 hardcover edition
ISBN 13: 978-1-59707-009-6 hardcover edition
ISBN: 1-59961-059-0 library bound edition

All Spotlight books are reinforced library binding and manufactured in the United States of America.

The Old Fashioned Mystery
of the Haunted Dollhouse

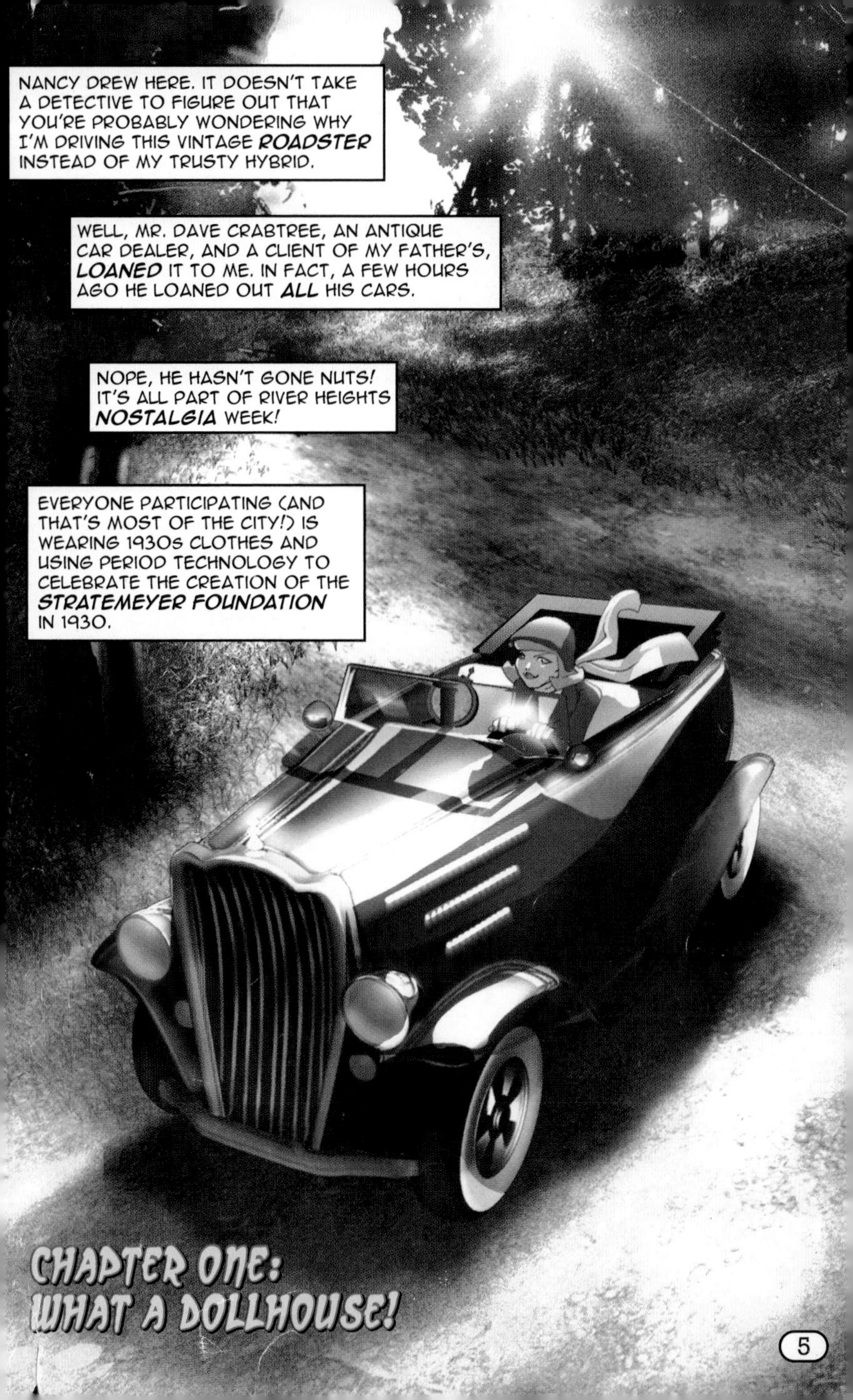

NANCY DREW HERE. IT DOESN'T TAKE A DETECTIVE TO FIGURE OUT THAT YOU'RE PROBABLY WONDERING WHY I'M DRIVING THIS VINTAGE *ROADSTER* INSTEAD OF MY TRUSTY HYBRID.
WELL, MR. DAVE CRABTREE, AN ANTIQUE CAR DEALER, AND A CLIENT OF MY FATHER'S, *LOANED* IT TO ME. IN FACT, A FEW HOURS AGO HE LOANED OUT *ALL* HIS CARS.
NOPE, HE HASN'T GONE NUTS! IT'S ALL PART OF RIVER HEIGHTS *NOSTALGIA* WEEK!
EVERYONE PARTICIPATING (AND THAT'S MOST OF THE CITY!) IS WEARING 1930s CLOTHES AND USING PERIOD TECHNOLOGY TO CELEBRATE THE CREATION OF THE *STRATEMEYER FOUNDATION* IN 1930.
CHAPTER ONE:
WHAT A DOLLHOUSE!

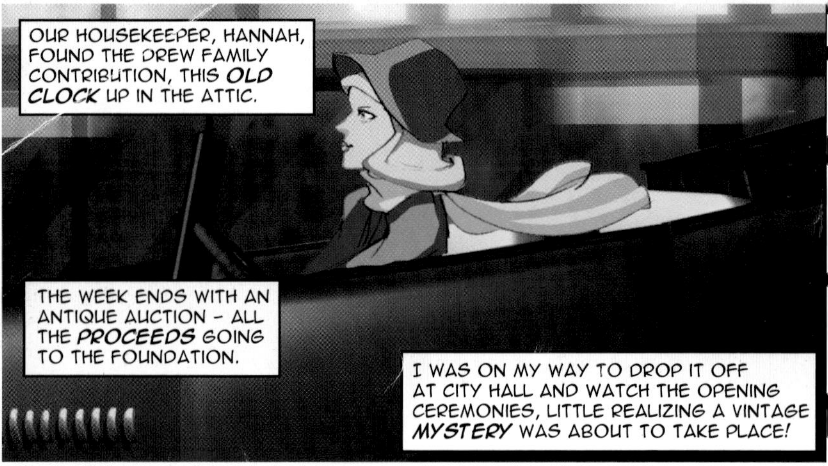
OUR HOUSEKEEPER, HANNAH, FOUND THE DREW FAMILY CONTRIBUTION, THIS OLD CLOCK UP IN THE ATTIC.
THE WEEK ENDS WITH AN ANTIQUE AUCTION - ALL THE PROCEEDS GOING TO THE FOUNDATION.
I WAS ON MY WAY TO DROP IT OFF AT CITY HALL AND WATCH THE OPENING CEREMONIES, LITTLE REALIZING A VINTAGE MYSTERY WAS ABOUT TO TAKE PLACE!

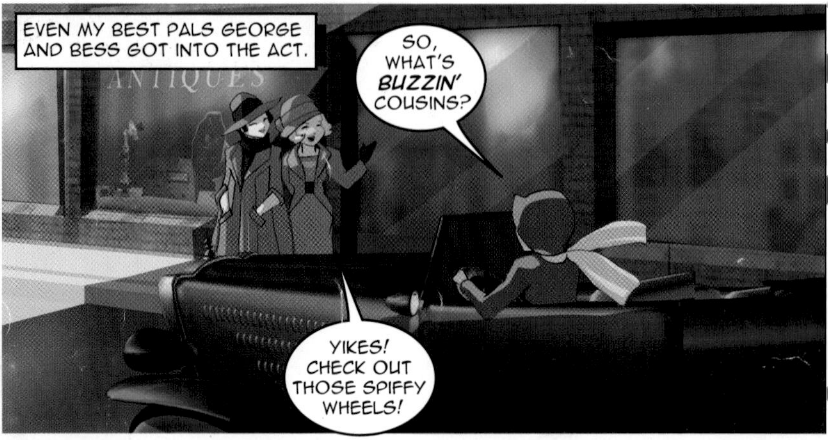
EVEN MY BEST PALS GEORGE AND BESS GOT INTO THE ACT.
ANTIQUES
SO, WHAT'S BUZZIN' COUSINS?
YIKES! CHECK OUT THOSE SPIFFY WHEELS!

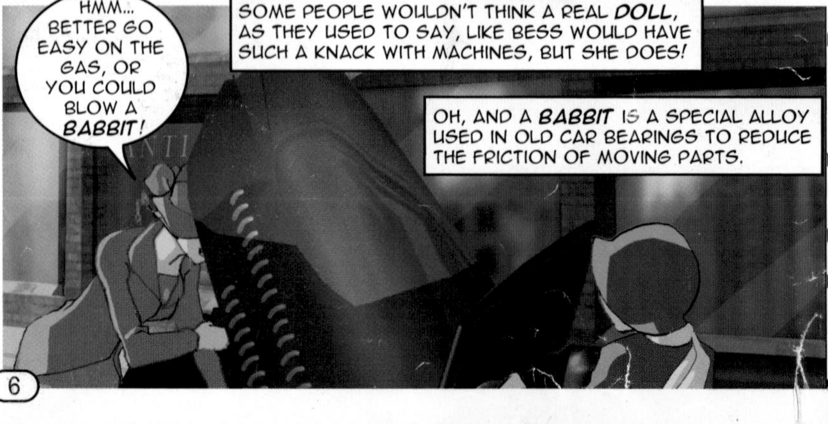
HMM... BETTER GO EASY ON THE GAS, OR YOU COULD BLOW A BABBIT!
SOME PEOPLE WOULDN'T THINK A REAL DOLL, AS THEY USED TO SAY, LIKE BESS WOULD HAVE SUCH A KNACK WITH MACHINES, BUT SHE DOES!
OH, AND A BABBIT IS A SPECIAL ALLOY USED IN OLD CAR BEARINGS TO REDUCE THE FRICTION OF MOVING PARTS.

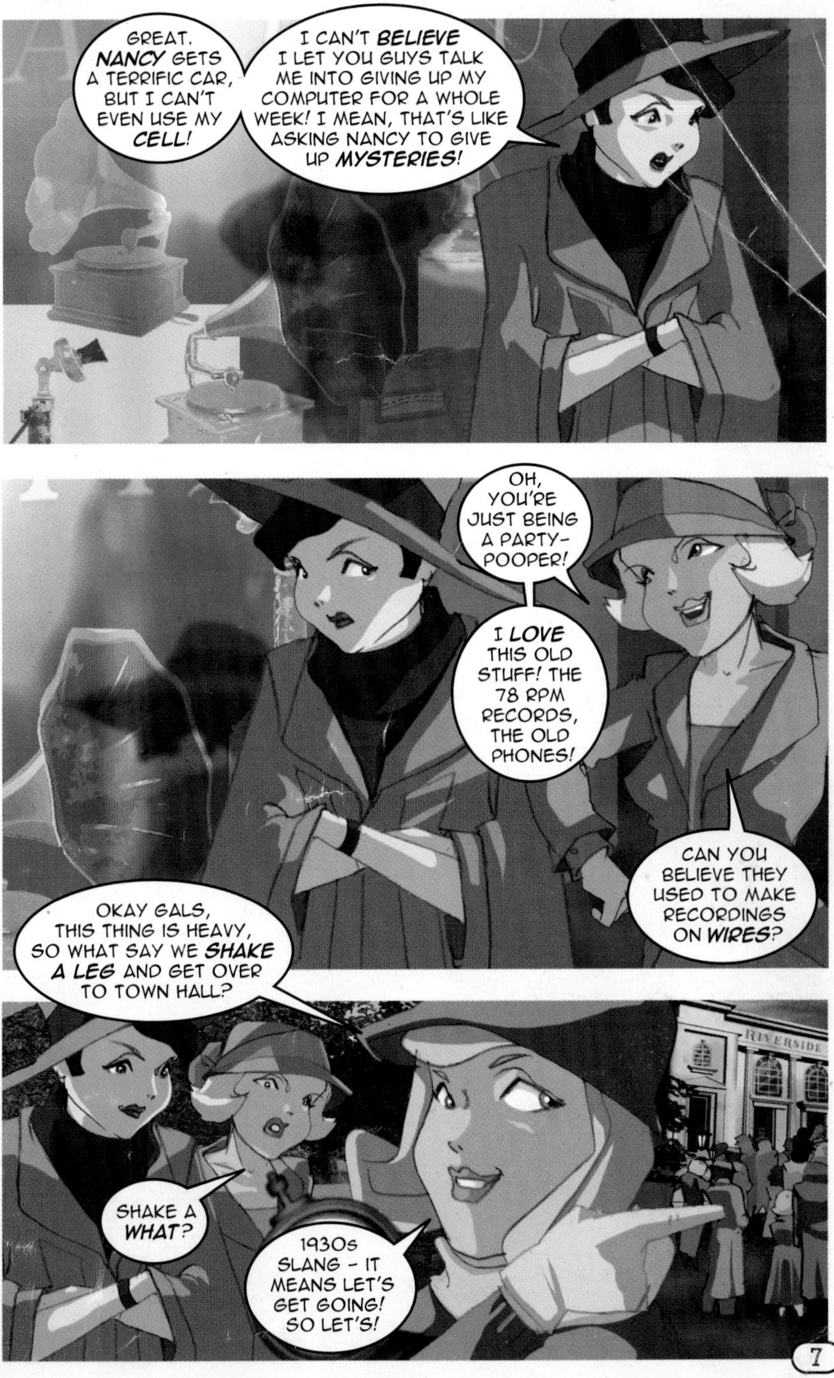
GREAT. NANCY GETS A TERRIFIC CAR, BUT I CAN'T EVEN USE MY CELL!
I CAN'T BELIEVE I LET YOU GUYS TALK ME INTO GIVING UP MY COMPUTER FOR A WHOLE WEEK! I MEAN, THAT'S LIKE ASKING NANCY TO GIVE UP MYSTERIES!
OH, YOU'RE JUST BEING A PARTY-POOPER!
I LOVE THIS OLD STUFF! THE 78 RPM RECORDS, THE OLD PHONES!
CAN YOU BELIEVE THEY USED TO MAKE RECORDINGS ON WIRES?
OKAY GALS, THIS THING IS HEAVY, SO WHAT SAY WE SHAKE A LEG AND GET OVER TO TOWN HALL?
RIVERSIDE
SHAKE A WHAT?
1930s SLANG – IT MEANS LET'S GET GOING! SO LET'S!

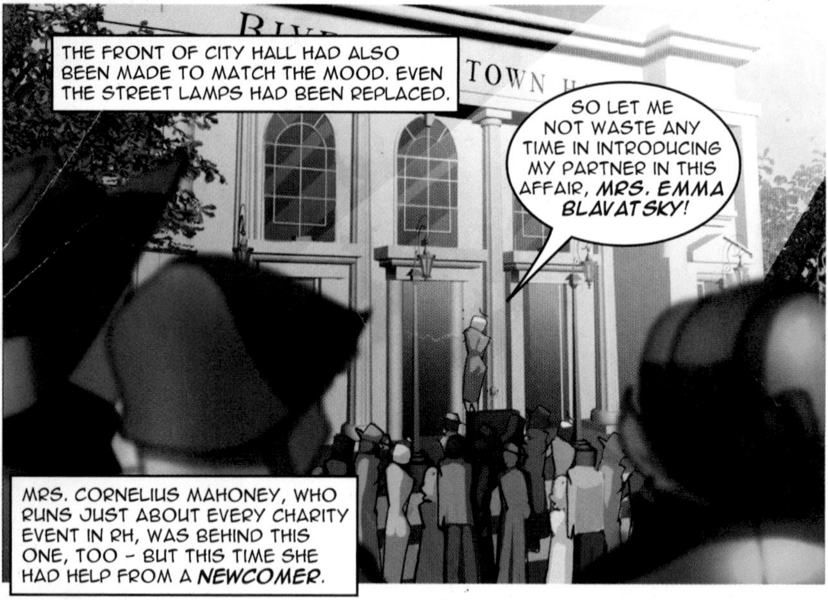
THE FRONT OF CITY HALL HAD ALSO BEEN MADE TO MATCH THE MOOD. EVEN THE STREET LAMPS HAD BEEN REPLACED.
SO LET ME NOT WASTE ANY TIME IN INTRODUCING MY PARTNER IN THIS AFFAIR, ***MRS. EMMA BLAVATSKY***!
MRS. CORNELIUS MAHONEY, WHO RUNS JUST ABOUT EVERY CHARITY EVENT IN RH, WAS BEHIND THIS ONE, TOO - BUT THIS TIME SHE HAD HELP FROM A ***NEWCOMER***.

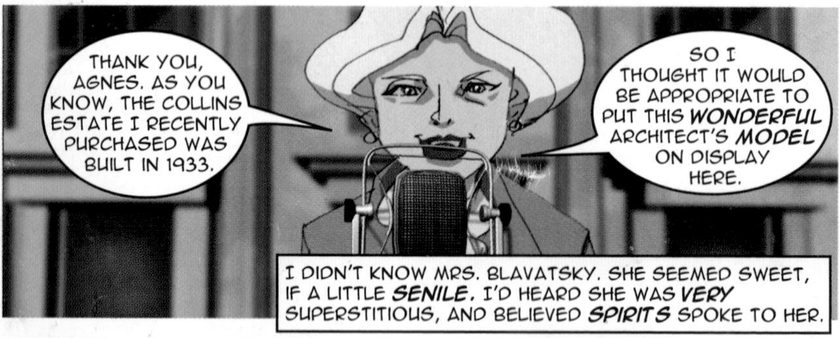
THANK YOU, AGNES. AS YOU KNOW, THE COLLINS ESTATE I RECENTLY PURCHASED WAS BUILT IN 1933.
SO I THOUGHT IT WOULD BE APPROPRIATE TO PUT THIS ***WONDERFUL*** ARCHITECT'S ***MODEL*** ON DISPLAY HERE.
I DIDN'T KNOW MRS. BLAVATSKY. SHE SEEMED SWEET, IF A LITTLE ***SENILE.*** I'D HEARD SHE WAS ***VERY*** SUPERSTITIOUS, AND BELIEVED ***SPIRITS*** SPOKE TO HER.

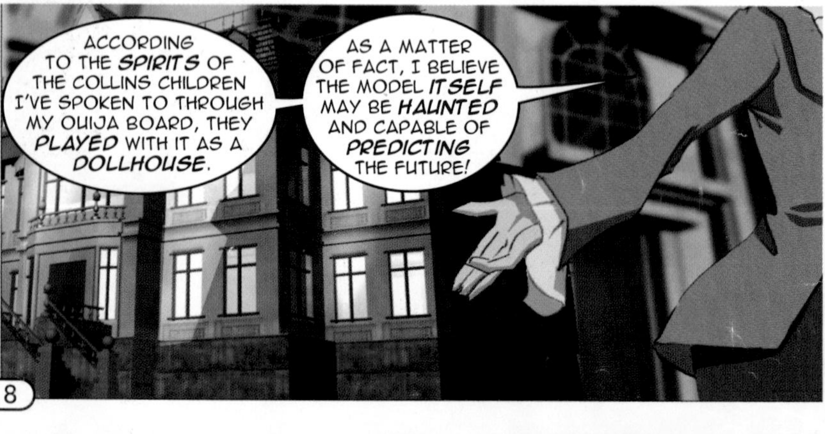
ACCORDING TO THE ***SPIRITS*** OF THE COLLINS CHILDREN I'VE SPOKEN TO THROUGH MY OUIJA BOARD, THEY ***PLAYED*** WITH IT AS A ***DOLLHOUSE***.
AS A MATTER OF FACT, I BELIEVE THE MODEL ***ITSELF*** MAY BE ***HAUNTED*** AND CAPABLE OF ***PREDICTING*** THE FUTURE!

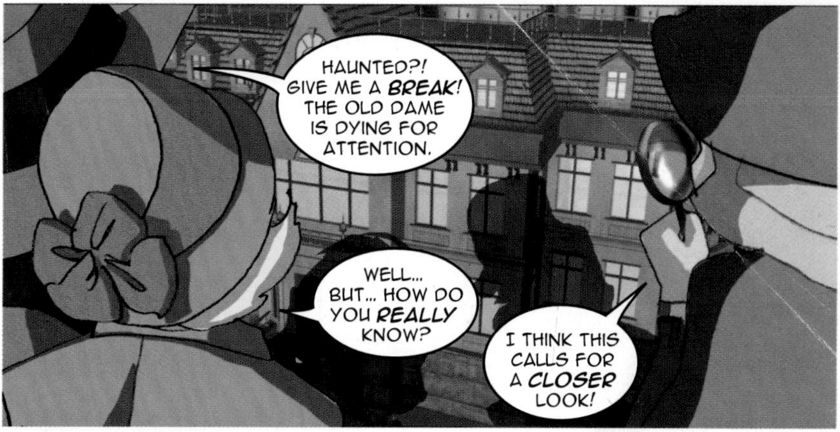
HAUNTED?! GIVE ME A BREAK! THE OLD DAME IS DYING FOR ATTENTION.
WELL... BUT... HOW DO YOU REALLY KNOW?
I THINK THIS CALLS FOR A CLOSER LOOK!

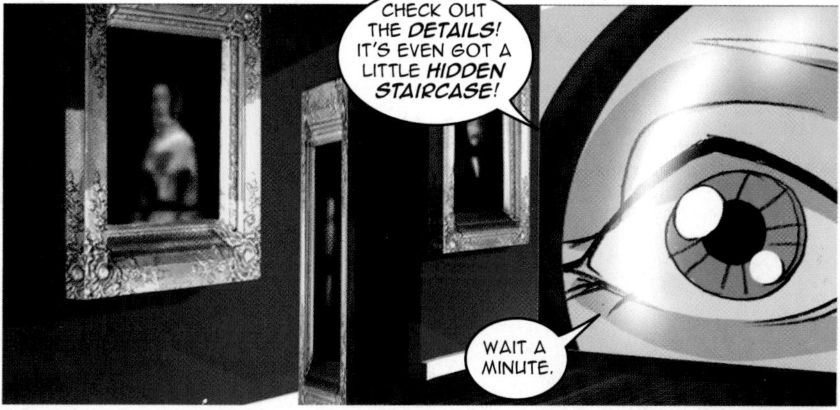
CHECK OUT THE DETAILS! IT'S EVEN GOT A LITTLE HIDDEN STAIRCASE!
WAIT A MINUTE.

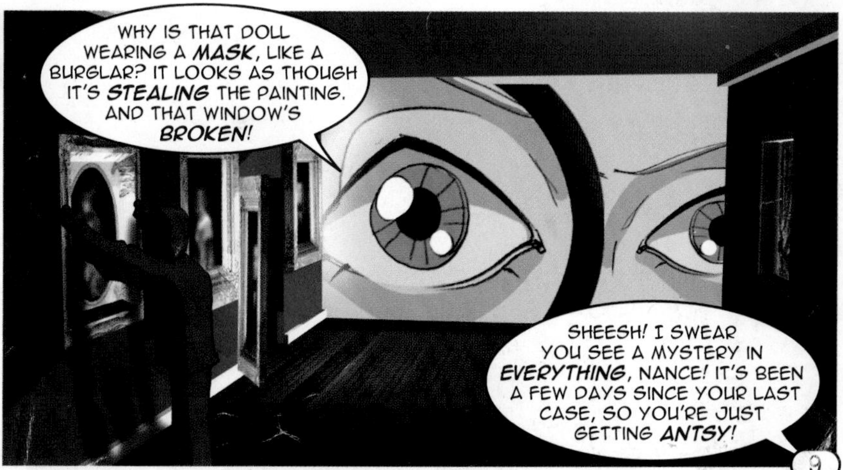
WHY IS THAT DOLL WEARING A MASK, LIKE A BURGLAR? IT LOOKS AS THOUGH IT'S STEALING THE PAINTING. AND THAT WINDOW'S BROKEN!
SHEESH! I SWEAR YOU SEE A MYSTERY IN EVERYTHING, NANCE! IT'S BEEN A FEW DAYS SINCE YOUR LAST CASE, SO YOU'RE JUST GETTING ANTSY!

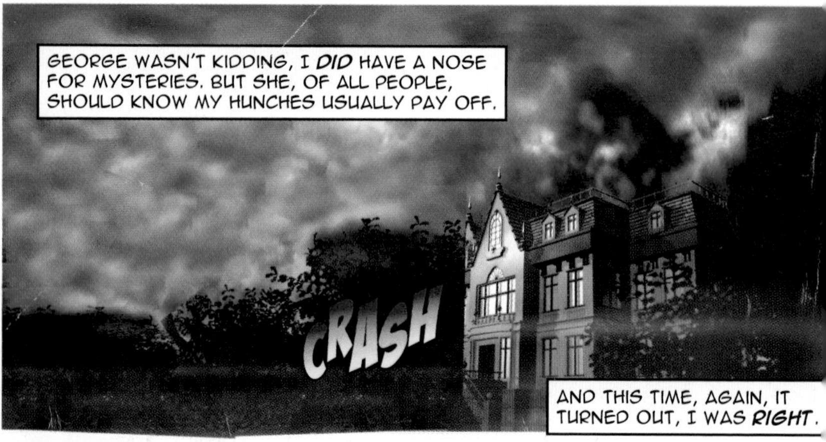
GEORGE WASN'T KIDDING, I DID HAVE A NOSE FOR MYSTERIES. BUT SHE, OF ALL PEOPLE, SHOULD KNOW MY HUNCHES USUALLY PAY OFF.
CRASH
AND THIS TIME, AGAIN, IT TURNED OUT, I WAS RIGHT.

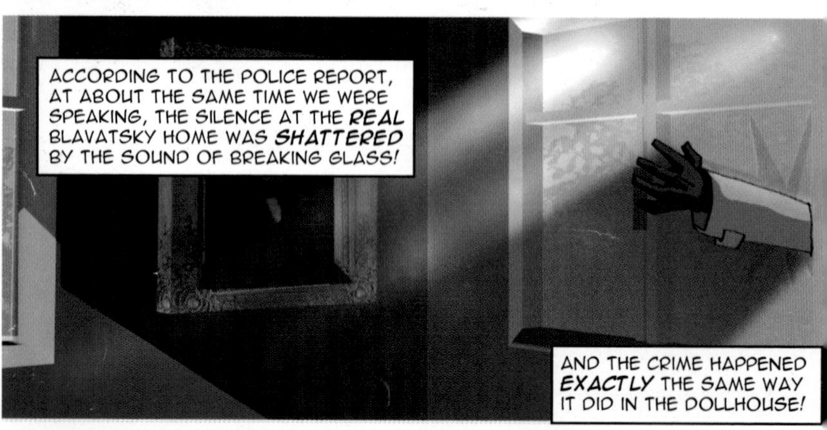
ACCORDING TO THE POLICE REPORT, AT ABOUT THE SAME TIME WE WERE SPEAKING, THE SILENCE AT THE REAL BLAVATSKY HOME WAS SHATTERED BY THE SOUND OF BREAKING GLASS!
AND THE CRIME HAPPENED EXACTLY THE SAME WAY IT DID IN THE DOLLHOUSE!

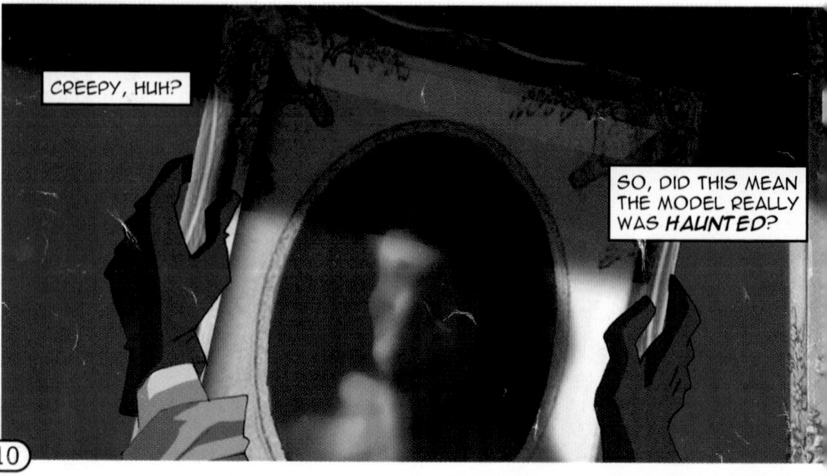
CREEPY, HUH?
SO, DID THIS MEAN THE MODEL REALLY WAS HAUNTED?

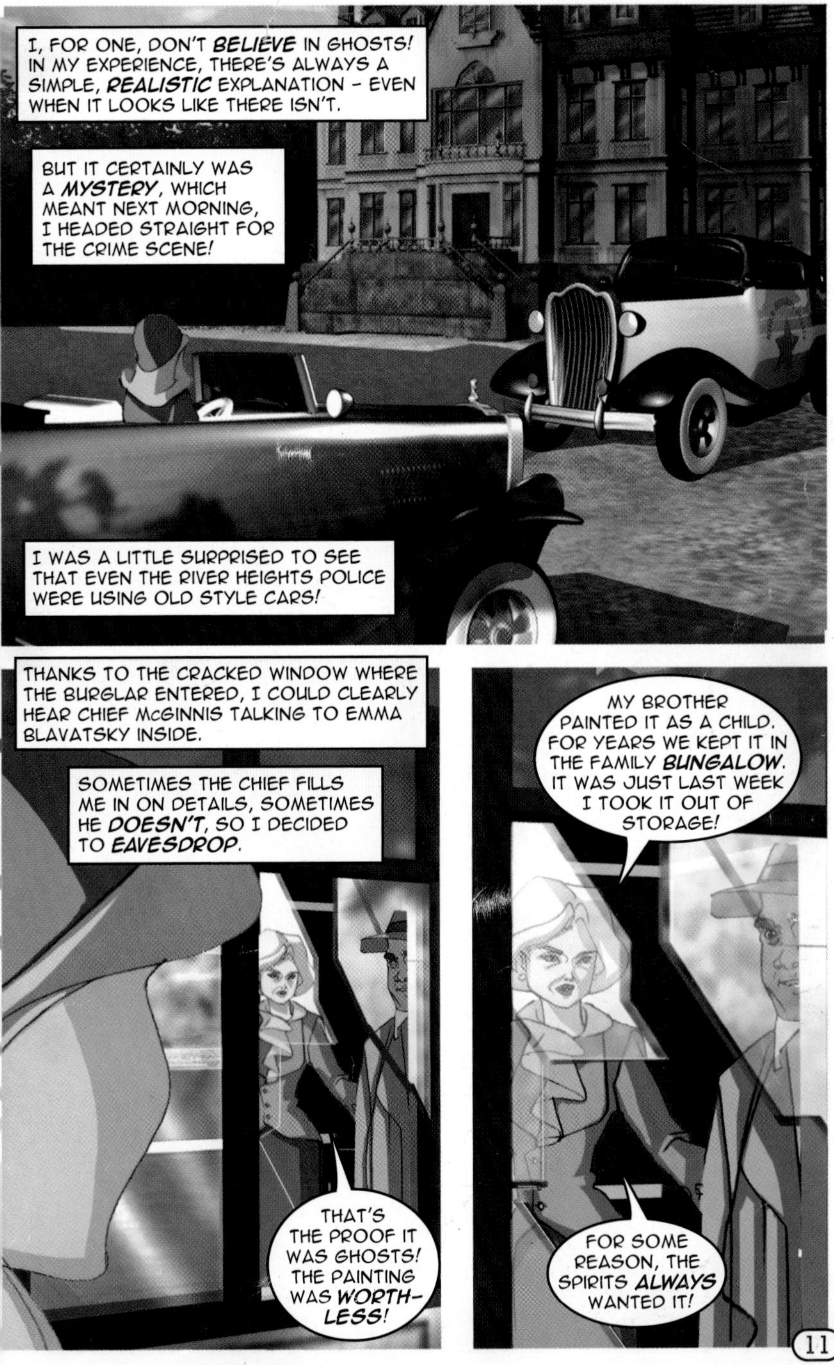
I, FOR ONE, DON'T *BELIEVE* IN GHOSTS! IN MY EXPERIENCE, THERE'S ALWAYS A SIMPLE, *REALISTIC* EXPLANATION - EVEN WHEN IT LOOKS LIKE THERE ISN'T.
BUT IT CERTAINLY WAS A *MYSTERY*, WHICH MEANT NEXT MORNING, I HEADED STRAIGHT FOR THE CRIME SCENE!
I WAS A LITTLE SURPRISED TO SEE THAT EVEN THE RIVER HEIGHTS POLICE WERE USING OLD STYLE CARS!
THANKS TO THE CRACKED WINDOW WHERE THE BURGLAR ENTERED, I COULD CLEARLY HEAR CHIEF McGINNIS TALKING TO EMMA BLAVATSKY INSIDE.
SOMETIMES THE CHIEF FILLS ME IN ON DETAILS, SOMETIMES HE *DOESN'T*, SO I DECIDED TO *EAVESDROP*.
THAT'S THE PROOF IT WAS GHOSTS! THE PAINTING WAS *WORTHLESS*!
MY BROTHER PAINTED IT AS A CHILD. FOR YEARS WE KEPT IT IN THE FAMILY *BUNGALOW*. IT WAS JUST LAST WEEK I TOOK IT OUT OF STORAGE!
FOR SOME REASON, THE SPIRITS *ALWAYS* WANTED IT!

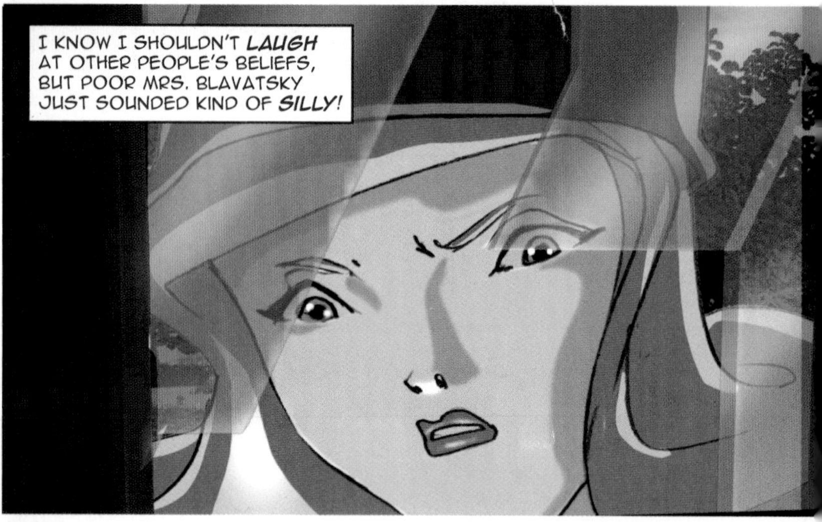
I KNOW I SHOULDN'T LAUGH AT OTHER PEOPLE'S BELIEFS, BUT POOR MRS. BLAVATSKY JUST SOUNDED KIND OF SILLY!

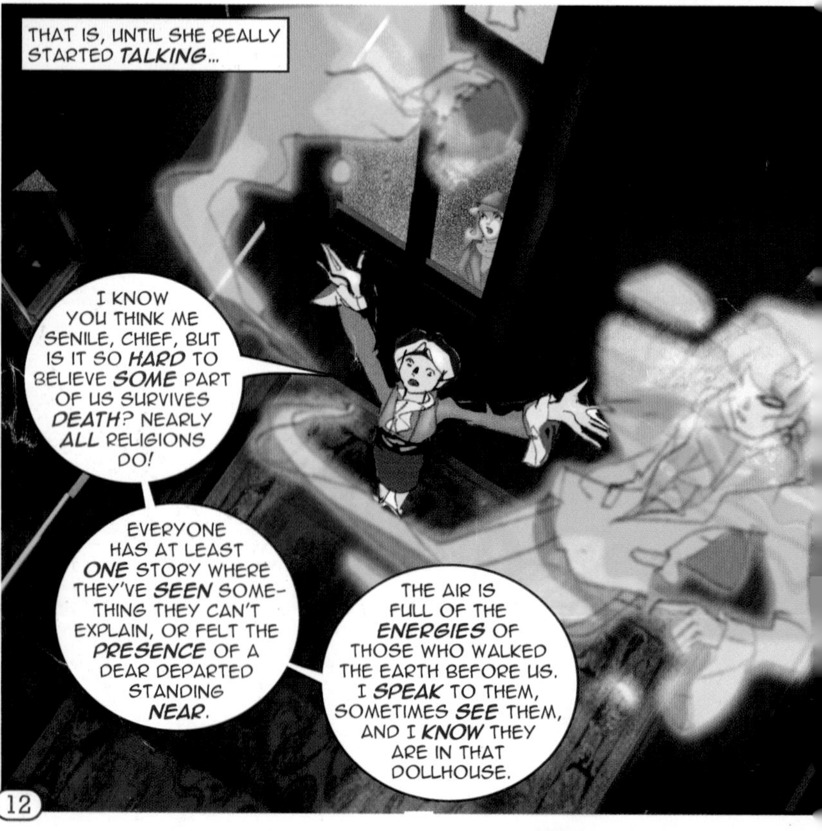
THAT IS, UNTIL SHE REALLY STARTED TALKING...
I KNOW YOU THINK ME SENILE, CHIEF, BUT IS IT SO HARD TO BELIEVE SOME PART OF US SURVIVES DEATH? NEARLY ALL RELIGIONS DO!
EVERYONE HAS AT LEAST ONE STORY WHERE THEY'VE SEEN SOME-THING THEY CAN'T EXPLAIN, OR FELT THE PRESENCE OF A DEAR DEPARTED STANDING NEAR.
THE AIR IS FULL OF THE ENERGIES OF THOSE WHO WALKED THE EARTH BEFORE US. I SPEAK TO THEM, SOMETIMES SEE THEM, AND I KNOW THEY ARE IN THAT DOLLHOUSE.

WHY *NOT* BELIEVE THE VEIL BETWEEN OUR WORLDS SOMETIMES GROWS *THIN*, SOME LOST SOUL CAN SLIP THROUGH, AND THE *PAST* COME TO LIFE?

HE SOUNDED SO SINCERE, HE HAD *ME* WONDERING IF SOME GHOST MIGHT BE STANDING RIGHT NEXT TO ME!

BOO!

AHHHH!

HA-HA-HA-HA!

SORRY, NANCY, I SAW YOU OUT HERE A WHILE AGO AND, SINCE I ALREADY FEEL LIKE I'M DRESSED FOR HALLOWEEN, I COULDN'T *RESIST* GIVING YOU A LITTLE *SCARE!*

SINCE YOU'RE HERE, WHY DON'T YOU COME INSIDE? MRS. BLAVATSKY HAS ALREADY *ASKED* FOR YOU!

I WAS THINKING ABOUT MENTIONING HOW *STRANGE* HE LOOKED IN HIS OLD HAT, BUT DECIDED THAT I SHOULDN'T — ESPECIALLY SINCE HE WAS LETTING ME INTO THE CRIME SCENE!

13

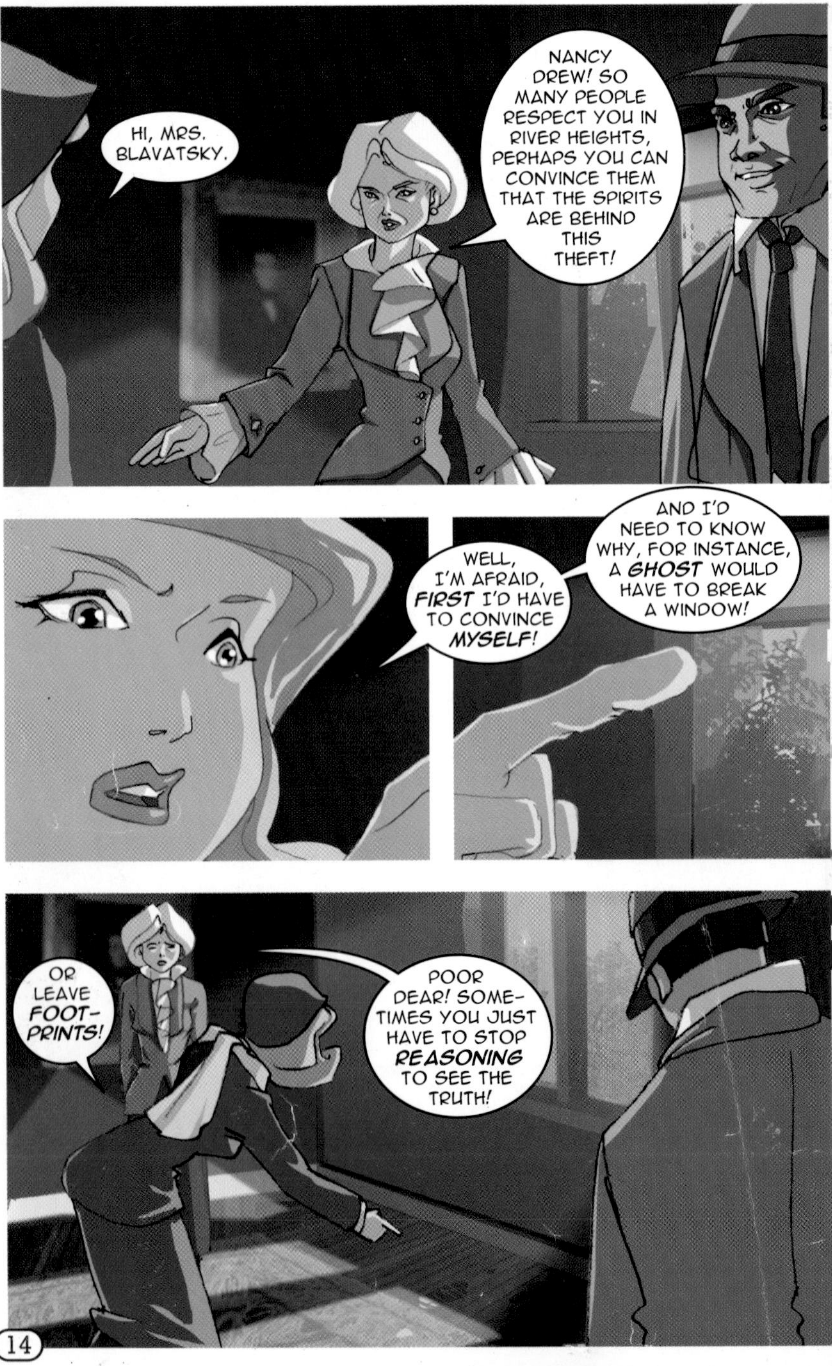
HI, MRS. BLAVATSKY.
NANCY DREW! SO MANY PEOPLE RESPECT YOU IN RIVER HEIGHTS, PERHAPS YOU CAN CONVINCE THEM THAT THE SPIRITS ARE BEHIND THIS THEFT!
WELL, I'M AFRAID, **FIRST** I'D HAVE TO CONVINCE **MYSELF**!
AND I'D NEED TO KNOW WHY, FOR INSTANCE, A **GHOST** WOULD HAVE TO BREAK A WINDOW!
OR LEAVE **FOOT-PRINTS**!
POOR DEAR! SOME-TIMES YOU JUST HAVE TO STOP **REASONING** TO SEE THE TRUTH!

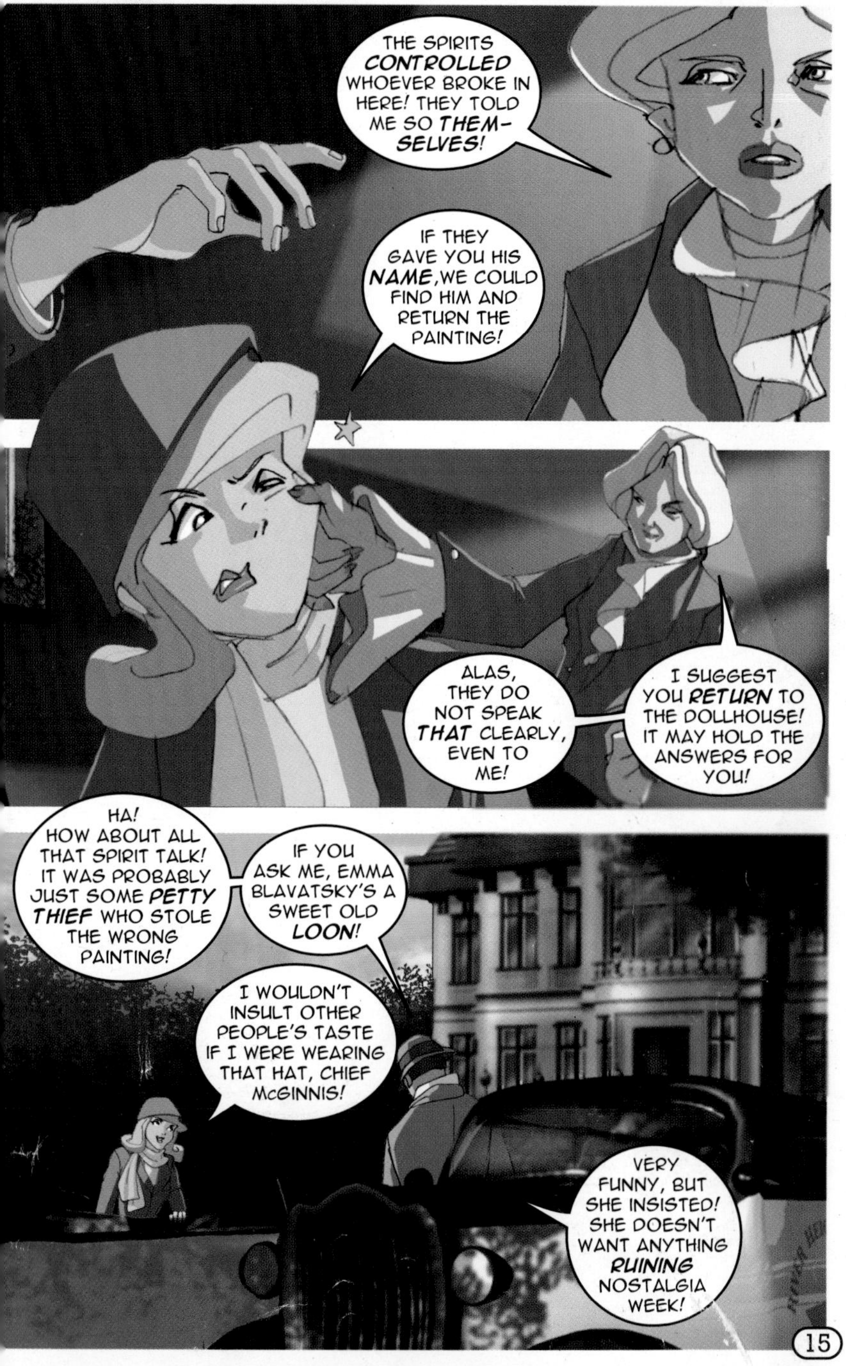
THE SPIRITS CONTROLLED WHOEVER BROKE IN HERE! THEY TOLD ME SO THEMSELVES!
IF THEY GAVE YOU HIS NAME, WE COULD FIND HIM AND RETURN THE PAINTING!
ALAS, THEY DO NOT SPEAK THAT CLEARLY, EVEN TO ME!
I SUGGEST YOU RETURN TO THE DOLLHOUSE! IT MAY HOLD THE ANSWERS FOR YOU!
HA! HOW ABOUT ALL THAT SPIRIT TALK! IT WAS PROBABLY JUST SOME PETTY THIEF WHO STOLE THE WRONG PAINTING!
IF YOU ASK ME, EMMA BLAVATSKY'S A SWEET OLD LOON!
I WOULDN'T INSULT OTHER PEOPLE'S TASTE IF I WERE WEARING THAT HAT, CHIEF McGINNIS!
VERY FUNNY, BUT SHE INSISTED! SHE DOESN'T WANT ANYTHING RUINING NOSTALGIA WEEK!

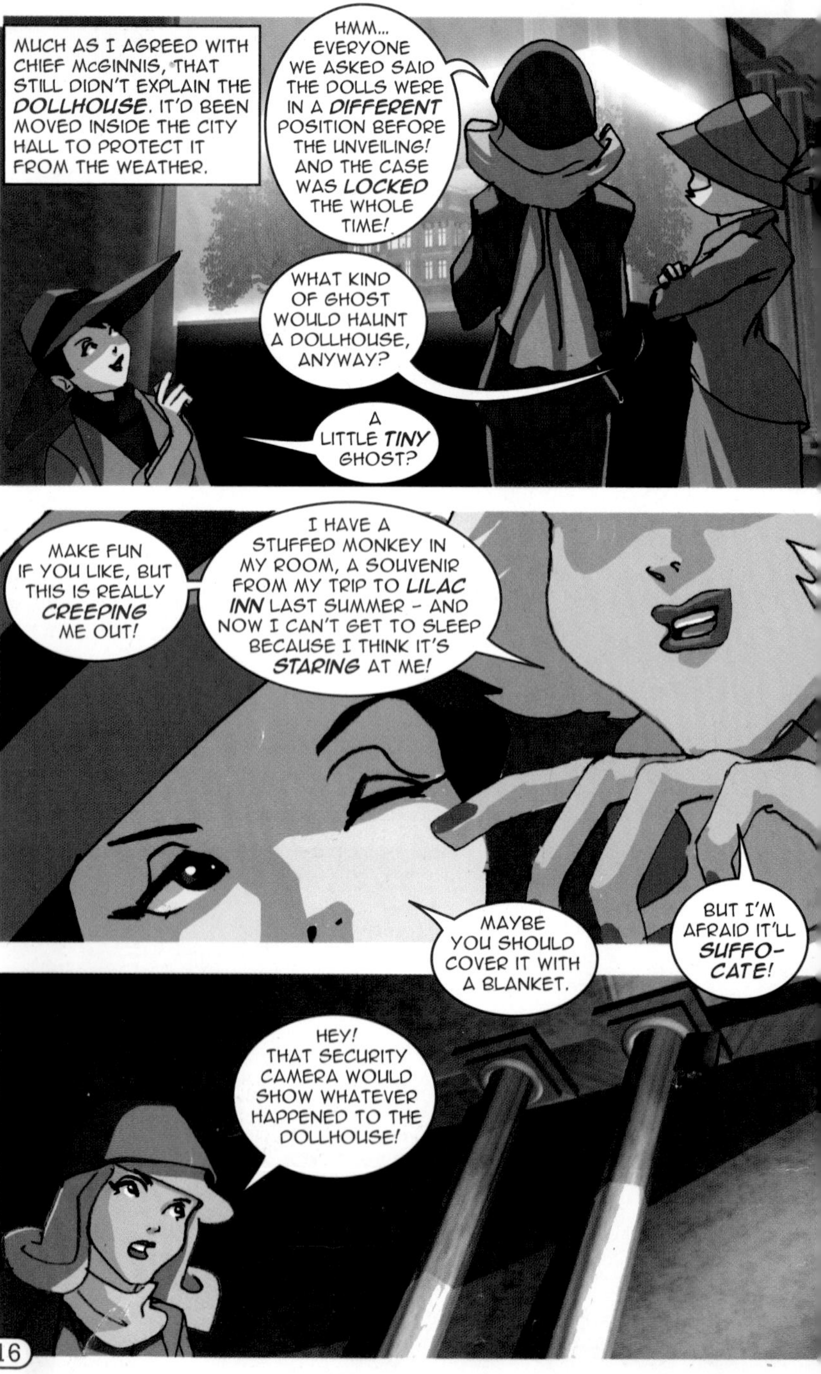
MUCH AS I AGREED WITH CHIEF McGINNIS, THAT STILL DIDN'T EXPLAIN THE DOLLHOUSE. IT'D BEEN MOVED INSIDE THE CITY HALL TO PROTECT IT FROM THE WEATHER.
HMM... EVERYONE WE ASKED SAID THE DOLLS WERE IN A DIFFERENT POSITION BEFORE THE UNVEILING! AND THE CASE WAS LOCKED THE WHOLE TIME!
WHAT KIND OF GHOST WOULD HAUNT A DOLLHOUSE, ANYWAY?
A LITTLE TINY GHOST?
MAKE FUN IF YOU LIKE, BUT THIS IS REALLY CREEPING ME OUT!
I HAVE A STUFFED MONKEY IN MY ROOM, A SOUVENIR FROM MY TRIP TO LILAC INN LAST SUMMER - AND NOW I CAN'T GET TO SLEEP BECAUSE I THINK IT'S STARING AT ME!
MAYBE YOU SHOULD COVER IT WITH A BLANKET.
BUT I'M AFRAID IT'LL SUFFO-CATE!
HEY! THAT SECURITY CAMERA WOULD SHOW WHATEVER HAPPENED TO THE DOLLHOUSE!

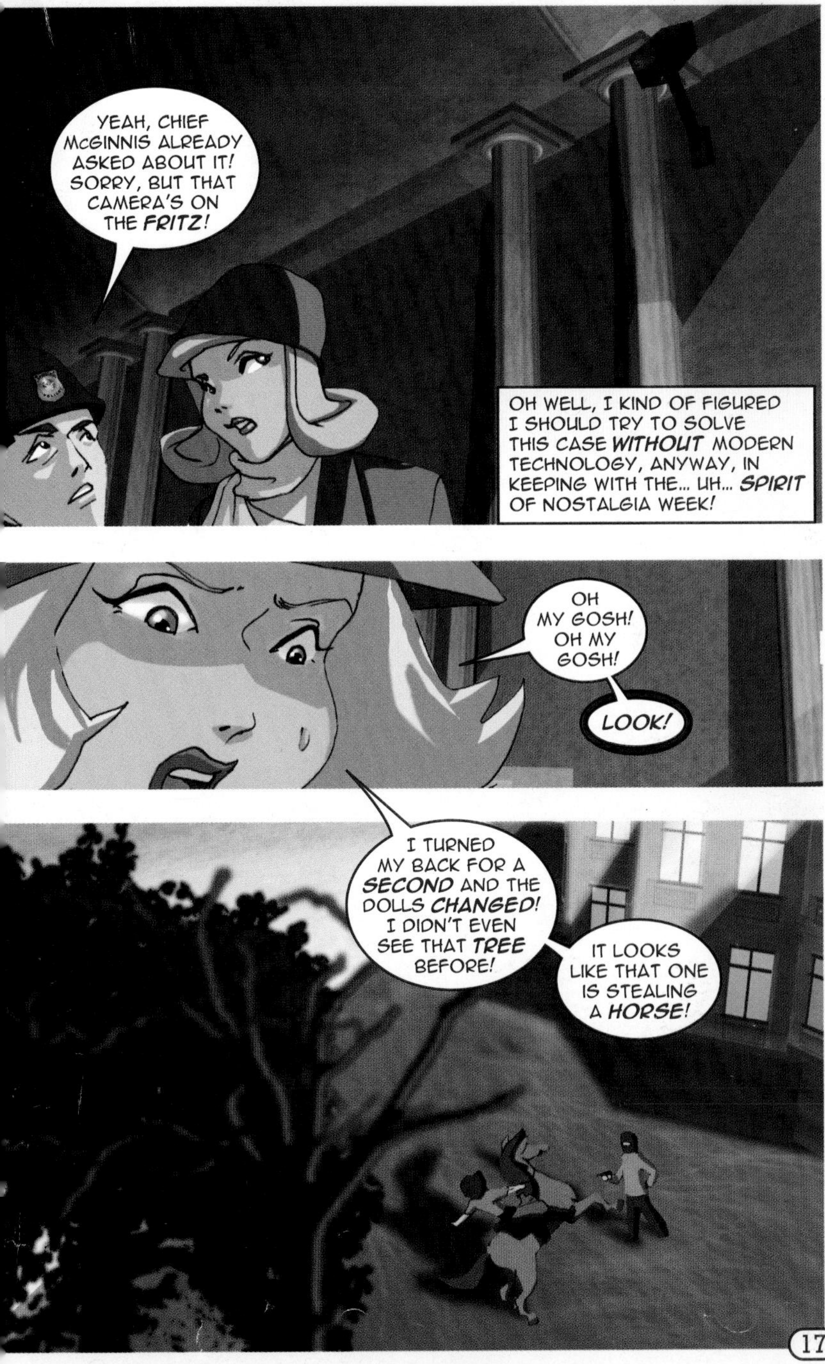
YEAH, CHIEF McGINNIS ALREADY ASKED ABOUT IT! SORRY, BUT THAT CAMERA'S ON THE FRITZ!
OH WELL, I KIND OF FIGURED I SHOULD TRY TO SOLVE THIS CASE WITHOUT MODERN TECHNOLOGY, ANYWAY, IN KEEPING WITH THE... UH... SPIRIT OF NOSTALGIA WEEK!
OH MY GOSH! OH MY GOSH!
LOOK!
I TURNED MY BACK FOR A SECOND AND THE DOLLS CHANGED! I DIDN'T EVEN SEE THAT TREE BEFORE!
IT LOOKS LIKE THAT ONE IS STEALING A HORSE!

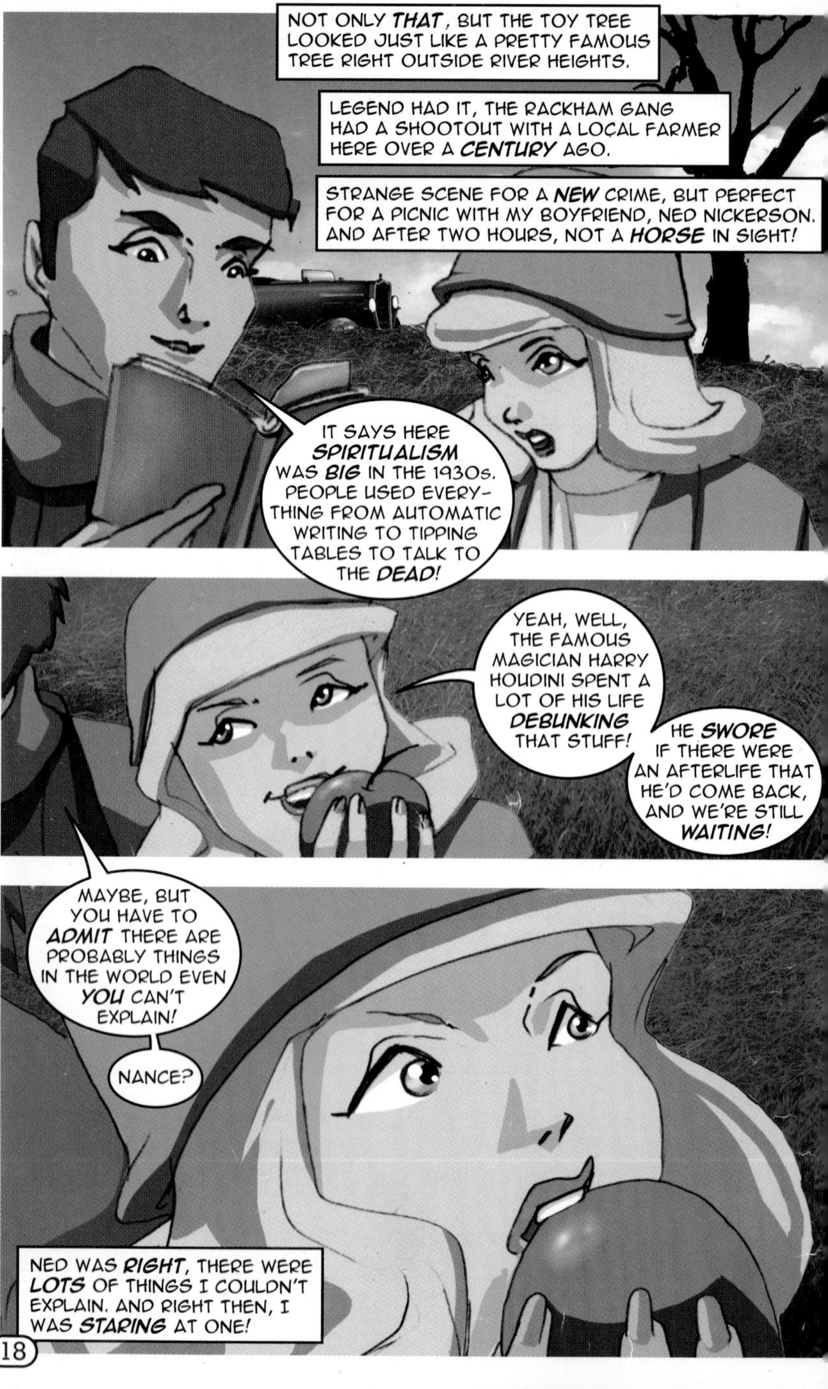

NOT ONLY THAT, BUT THE TOY TREE LOOKED JUST LIKE A PRETTY FAMOUS TREE RIGHT OUTSIDE RIVER HEIGHTS.
LEGEND HAD IT, THE RACKHAM GANG HAD A SHOOTOUT WITH A LOCAL FARMER HERE OVER A CENTURY AGO.
STRANGE SCENE FOR A NEW CRIME, BUT PERFECT FOR A PICNIC WITH MY BOYFRIEND, NED NICKERSON. AND AFTER TWO HOURS, NOT A HORSE IN SIGHT!
IT SAYS HERE SPIRITUALISM WAS BIG IN THE 1930s. PEOPLE USED EVERYTHING FROM AUTOMATIC WRITING TO TIPPING TABLES TO TALK TO THE DEAD!
YEAH, WELL, THE FAMOUS MAGICIAN HARRY HOUDINI SPENT A LOT OF HIS LIFE DEBUNKING THAT STUFF!
HE SWORE IF THERE WERE AN AFTERLIFE THAT HE'D COME BACK, AND WE'RE STILL WAITING!
MAYBE, BUT YOU HAVE TO ADMIT THERE ARE PROBABLY THINGS IN THE WORLD EVEN YOU CAN'T EXPLAIN!
NANCE?
NED WAS RIGHT, THERE WERE LOTS OF THINGS I COULDN'T EXPLAIN. AND RIGHT THEN, I WAS STARING AT ONE!

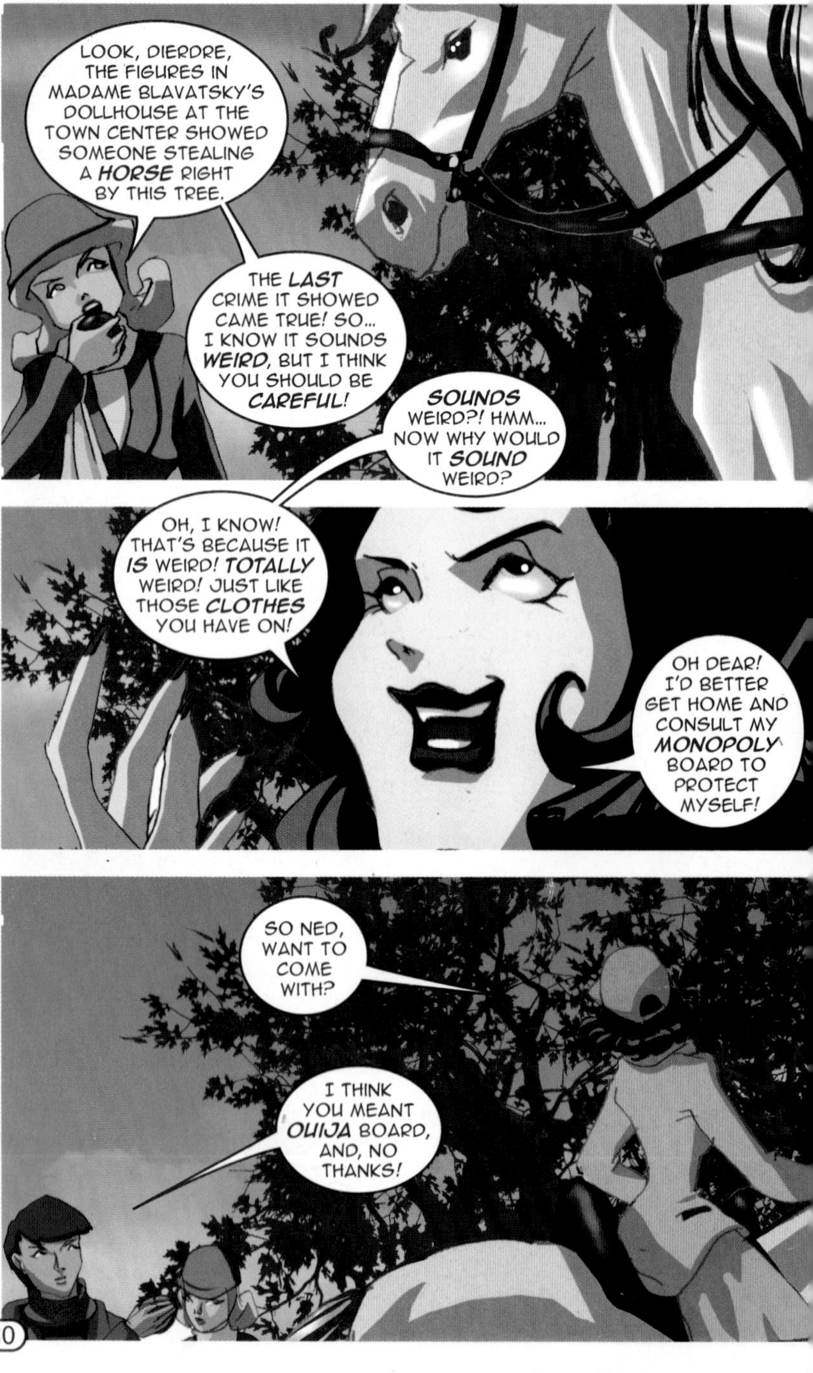
LOOK, DIERDRE, THE FIGURES IN MADAME BLAVATSKY'S DOLLHOUSE AT THE TOWN CENTER SHOWED SOMEONE STEALING A HORSE RIGHT BY THIS TREE.
THE LAST CRIME IT SHOWED CAME TRUE! SO... I KNOW IT SOUNDS WEIRD, BUT I THINK YOU SHOULD BE CAREFUL!
SOUNDS WEIRD?! HMM... NOW WHY WOULD IT SOUND WEIRD?
OH, I KNOW! THAT'S BECAUSE IT IS WEIRD! TOTALLY WEIRD! JUST LIKE THOSE CLOTHES YOU HAVE ON!
OH DEAR! I'D BETTER GET HOME AND CONSULT MY MONOPOLY BOARD TO PROTECT MYSELF!
SO NED, WANT TO COME WITH?
I THINK YOU MEANT OUIJA BOARD, AND, NO THANKS!

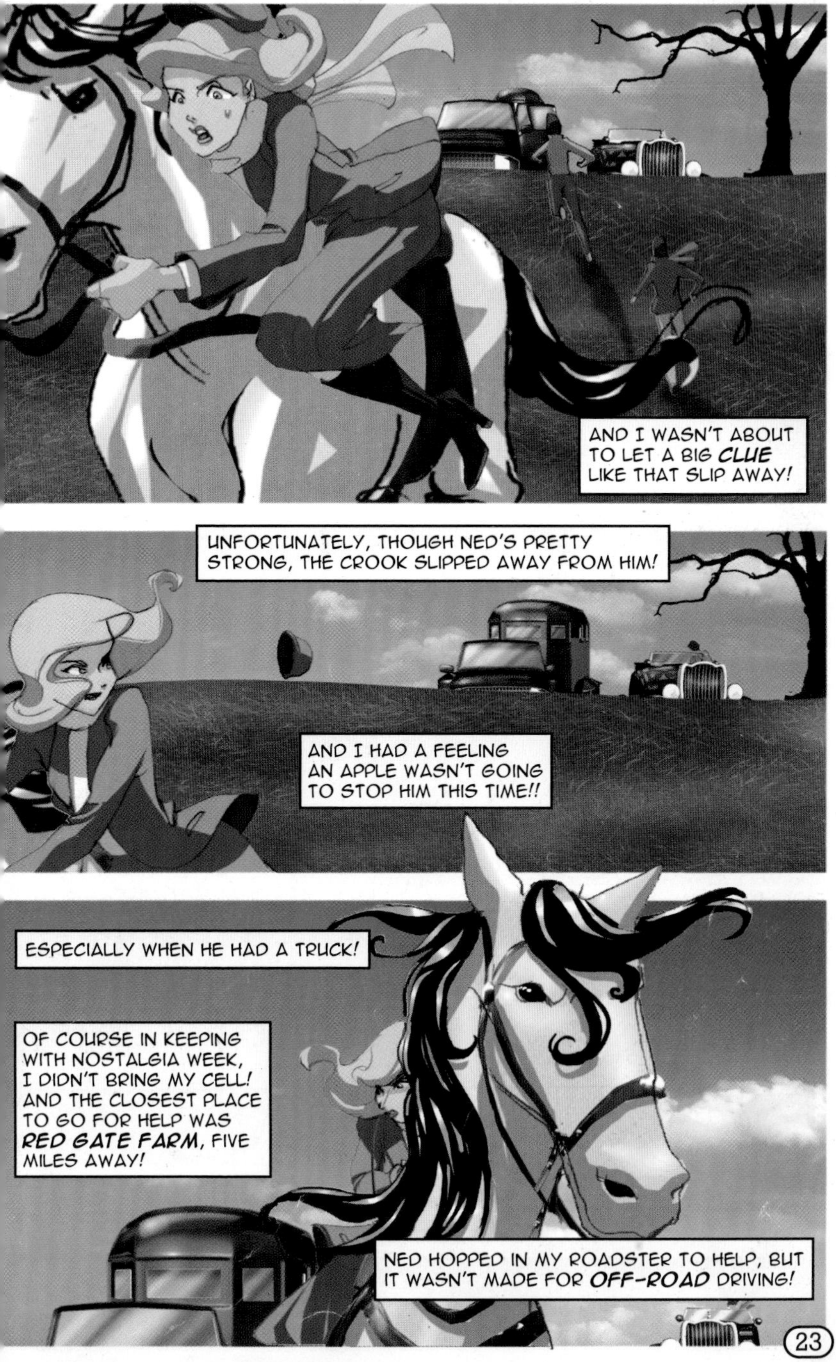
AND I WASN'T ABOUT TO LET A BIG CLUE LIKE THAT SLIP AWAY!
UNFORTUNATELY, THOUGH NED'S PRETTY STRONG, THE CROOK SLIPPED AWAY FROM HIM!
AND I HAD A FEELING AN APPLE WASN'T GOING TO STOP HIM THIS TIME!!
ESPECIALLY WHEN HE HAD A TRUCK!
OF COURSE IN KEEPING WITH NOSTALGIA WEEK, I DIDN'T BRING MY CELL! AND THE CLOSEST PLACE TO GO FOR HELP WAS RED GATE FARM, FIVE MILES AWAY!
NED HOPPED IN MY ROADSTER TO HELP, BUT IT WASN'T MADE FOR OFF-ROAD DRIVING!

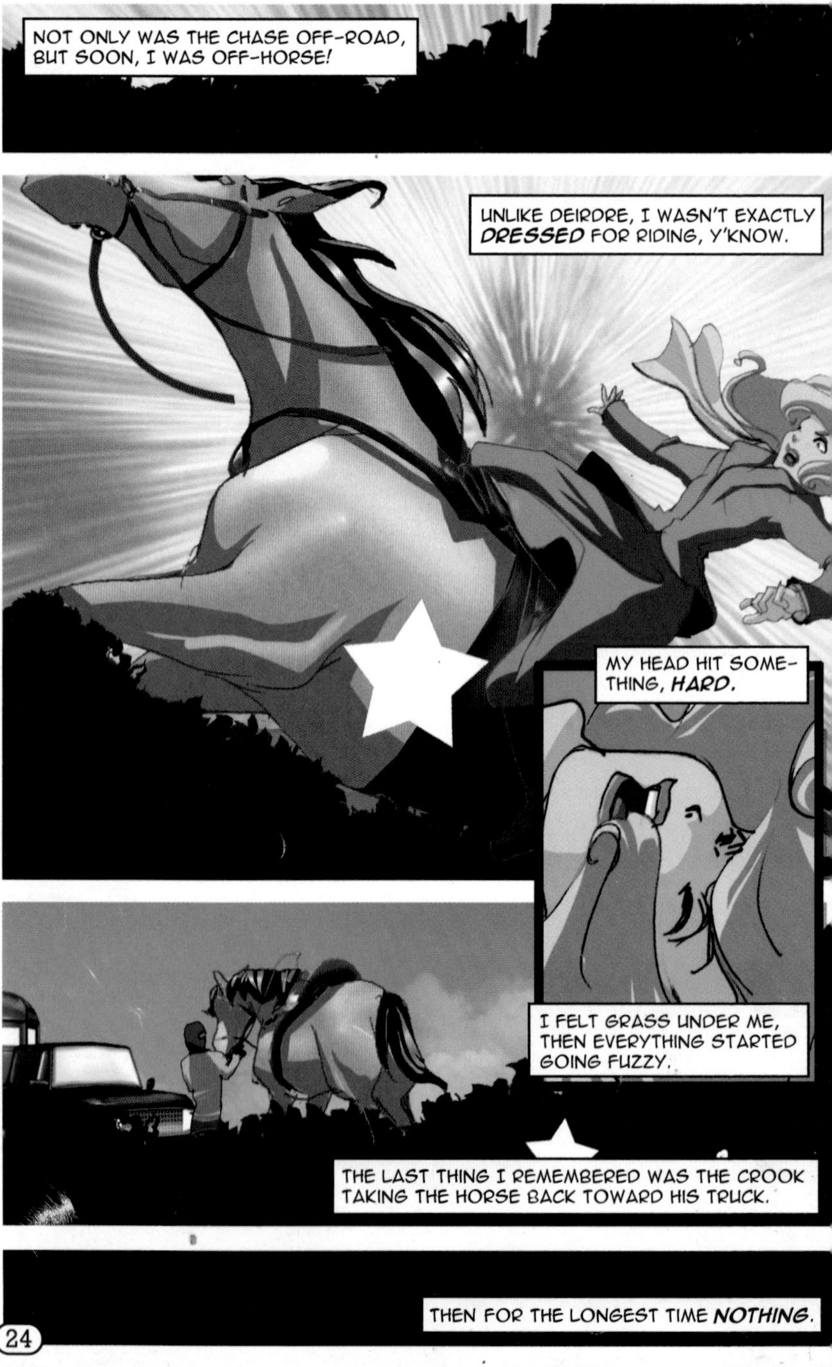
NOT ONLY WAS THE CHASE OFF-ROAD, BUT SOON, I WAS OFF-HORSE!
UNLIKE DEIRDRE, I WASN'T EXACTLY **DRESSED** FOR RIDING, Y'KNOW.
MY HEAD HIT SOME-THING, **HARD.**
I FELT GRASS UNDER ME, THEN EVERYTHING STARTED GOING FUZZY.
THE LAST THING I REMEMBERED WAS THE CROOK TAKING THE HORSE BACK TOWARD HIS TRUCK.
THEN FOR THE LONGEST TIME **NOTHING**.

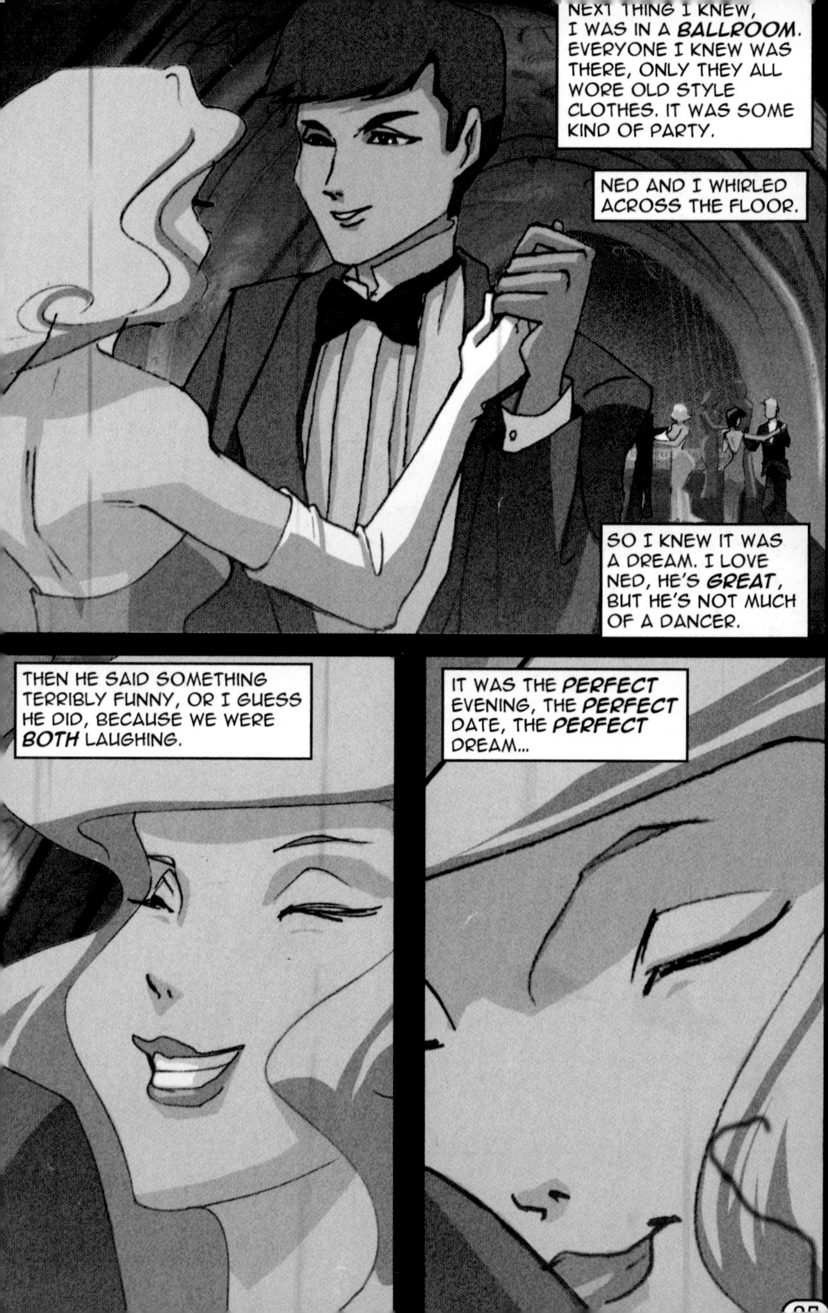
NEXT THING I KNEW, I WAS IN A BALLROOM. EVERYONE I KNEW WAS THERE, ONLY THEY ALL WORE OLD STYLE CLOTHES. IT WAS SOME KIND OF PARTY.
NED AND I WHIRLED ACROSS THE FLOOR.
SO I KNEW IT WAS A DREAM. I LOVE NED, HE'S GREAT, BUT HE'S NOT MUCH OF A DANCER.
THEN HE SAID SOMETHING TERRIBLY FUNNY, OR I GUESS HE DID, BECAUSE WE WERE BOTH LAUGHING.
IT WAS THE PERFECT EVENING, THE PERFECT DATE, THE PERFECT DREAM...

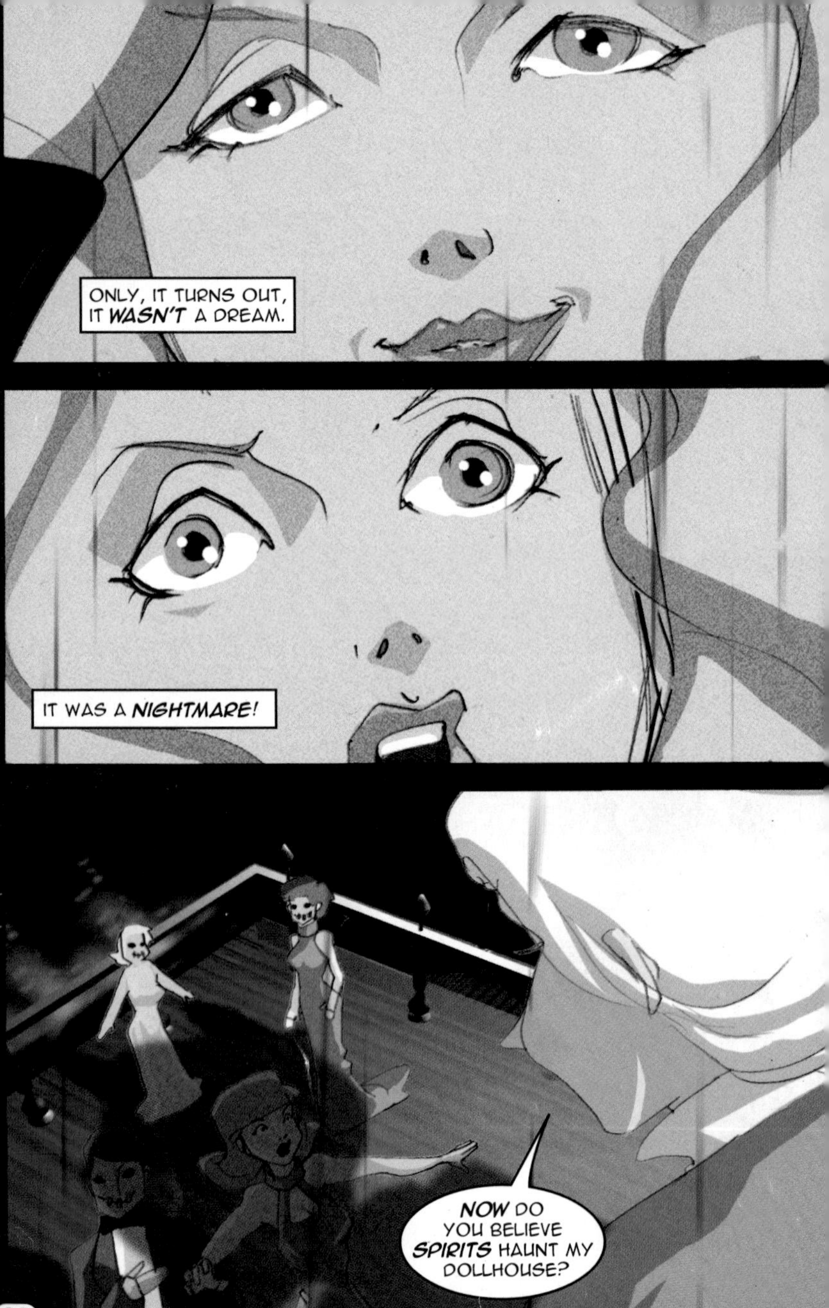
ONLY, IT TURNS OUT, IT WASN'T A DREAM.
IT WAS A NIGHTMARE!
NOW DO YOU BELIEVE SPIRITS HAUNT MY DOLLHOUSE?

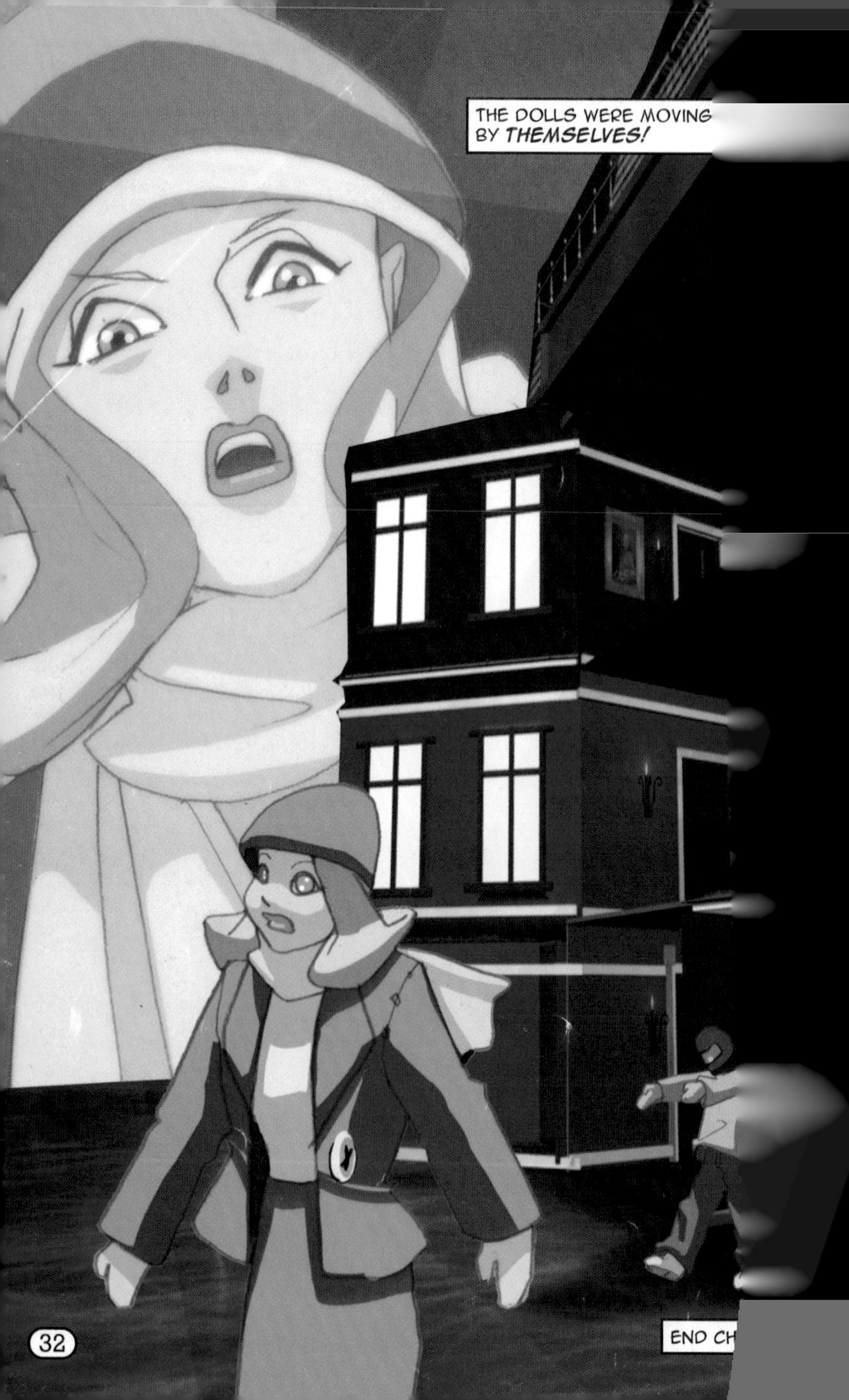
THE DOLLS WERE MOVING
BY THEMSELVES!
END CH

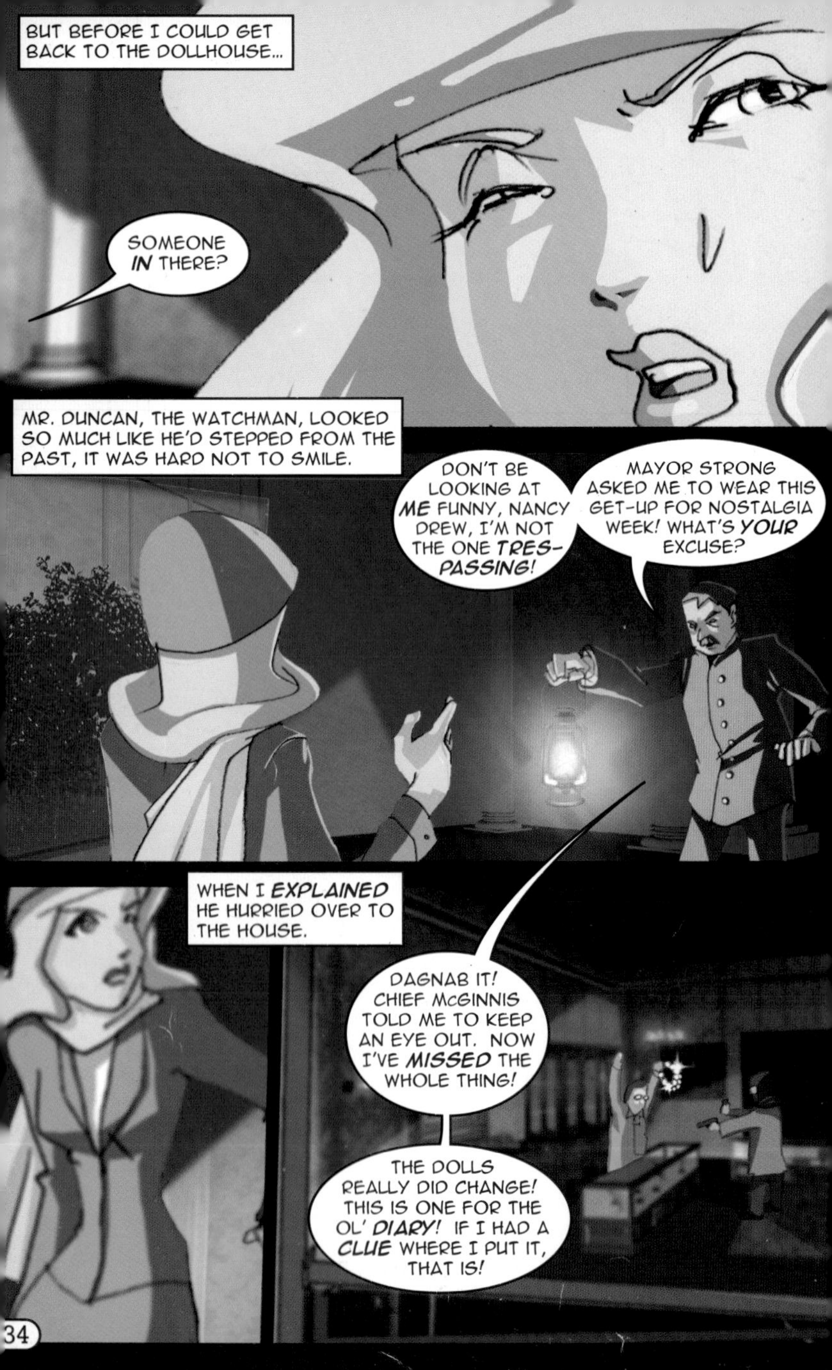

BUT BEFORE I COULD GET BACK TO THE DOLLHOUSE...
SOMEONE IN THERE?
MR. DUNCAN, THE WATCHMAN, LOOKED SO MUCH LIKE HE'D STEPPED FROM THE PAST, IT WAS HARD NOT TO SMILE.
DON'T BE LOOKING AT ME FUNNY, NANCY DREW, I'M NOT THE ONE TRES-PASSING!
MAYOR STRONG ASKED ME TO WEAR THIS GET-UP FOR NOSTALGIA WEEK! WHAT'S YOUR EXCUSE?
WHEN I EXPLAINED HE HURRIED OVER TO THE HOUSE.
DAGNAB IT! CHIEF McGINNIS TOLD ME TO KEEP AN EYE OUT. NOW I'VE MISSED THE WHOLE THING!
THE DOLLS REALLY DID CHANGE! THIS IS ONE FOR THE OL' DIARY! IF I HAD A CLUE WHERE I PUT IT, THAT IS!

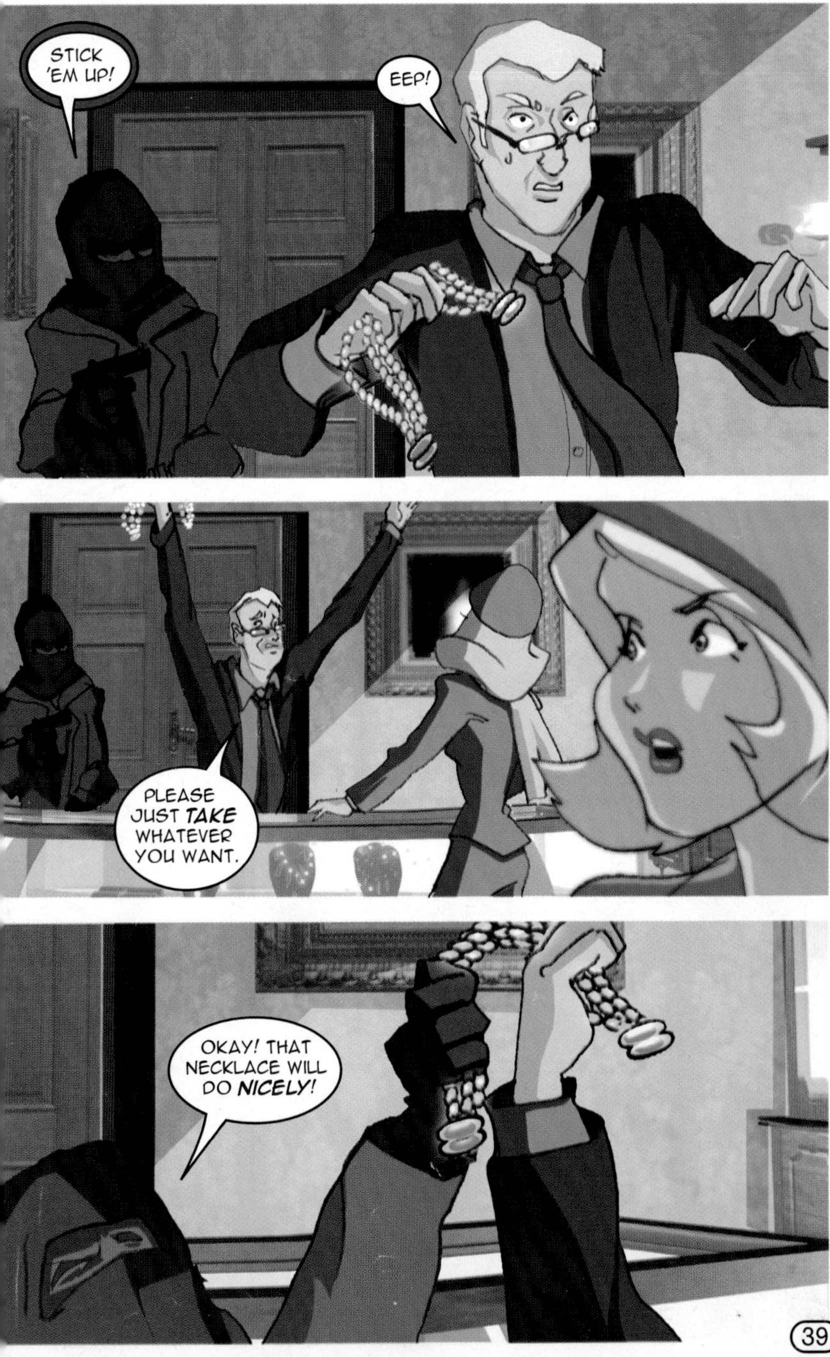
STICK 'EM UP!
EEP!
PLEASE JUST TAKE WHATEVER YOU WANT.
OKAY! THAT NECKLACE WILL DO NICELY!

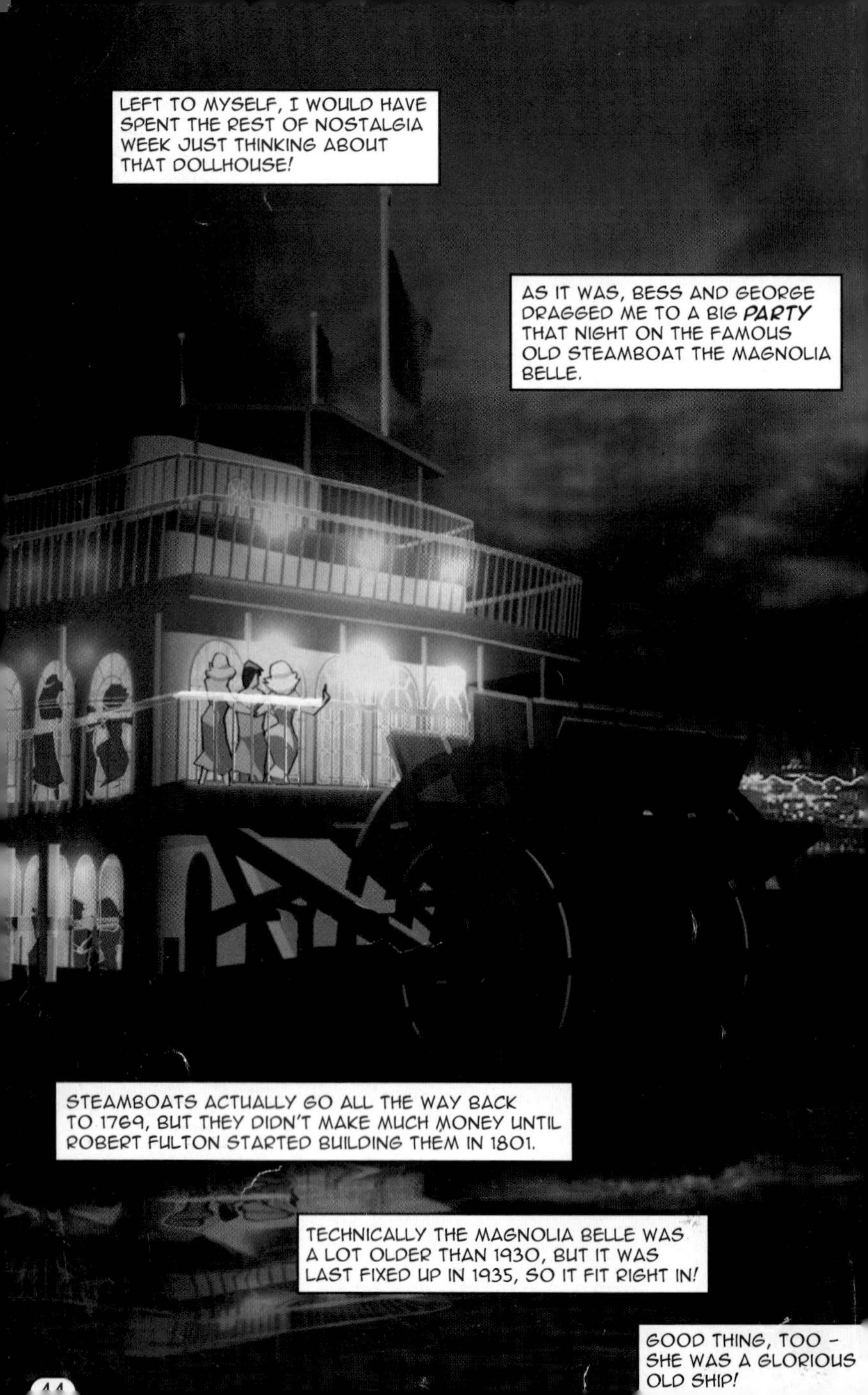
LEFT TO MYSELF, I WOULD HAVE SPENT THE REST OF NOSTALGIA WEEK JUST THINKING ABOUT THAT DOLLHOUSE!
AS IT WAS, BESS AND GEORGE DRAGGED ME TO A BIG PARTY THAT NIGHT ON THE FAMOUS OLD STEAMBOAT THE MAGNOLIA BELLE.
STEAMBOATS ACTUALLY GO ALL THE WAY BACK TO 1769, BUT THEY DIDN'T MAKE MUCH MONEY UNTIL ROBERT FULTON STARTED BUILDING THEM IN 1801.
TECHNICALLY THE MAGNOLIA BELLE WAS A LOT OLDER THAN 1930, BUT IT WAS LAST FIXED UP IN 1935, SO IT FIT RIGHT IN!
GOOD THING, TOO - SHE WAS A GLORIOUS OLD SHIP!

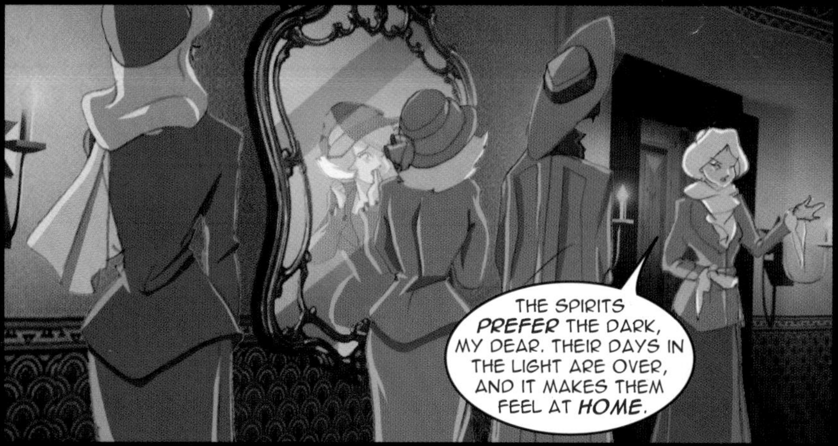
THE SPIRITS PREFER THE DARK, MY DEAR. THEIR DAYS IN THE LIGHT ARE OVER, AND IT MAKES THEM FEEL AT HOME.

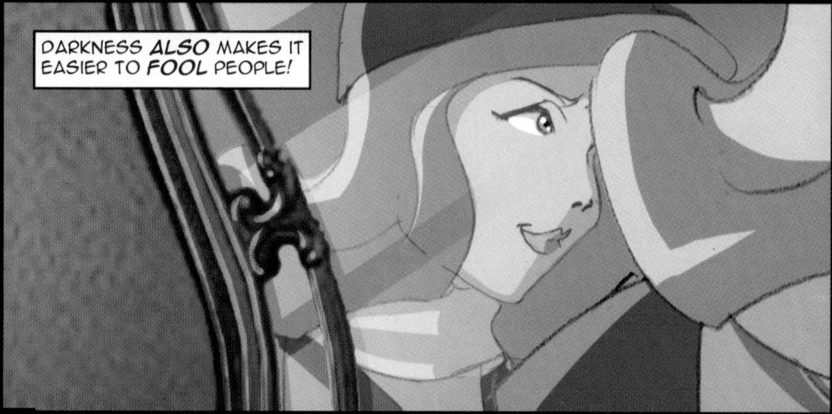
DARKNESS ALSO MAKES IT EASIER TO FOOL PEOPLE!

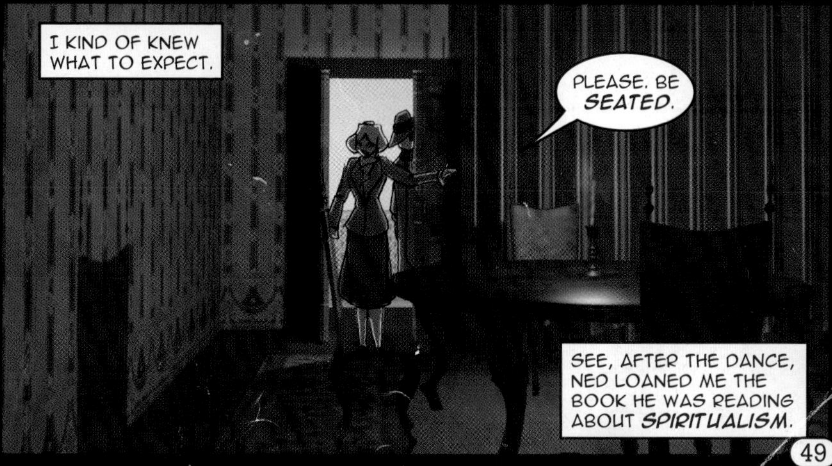
I KIND OF KNEW WHAT TO EXPECT.
PLEASE. BE SEATED.
SEE, AFTER THE DANCE, NED LOANED ME THE BOOK HE WAS READING ABOUT SPIRITUALISM.

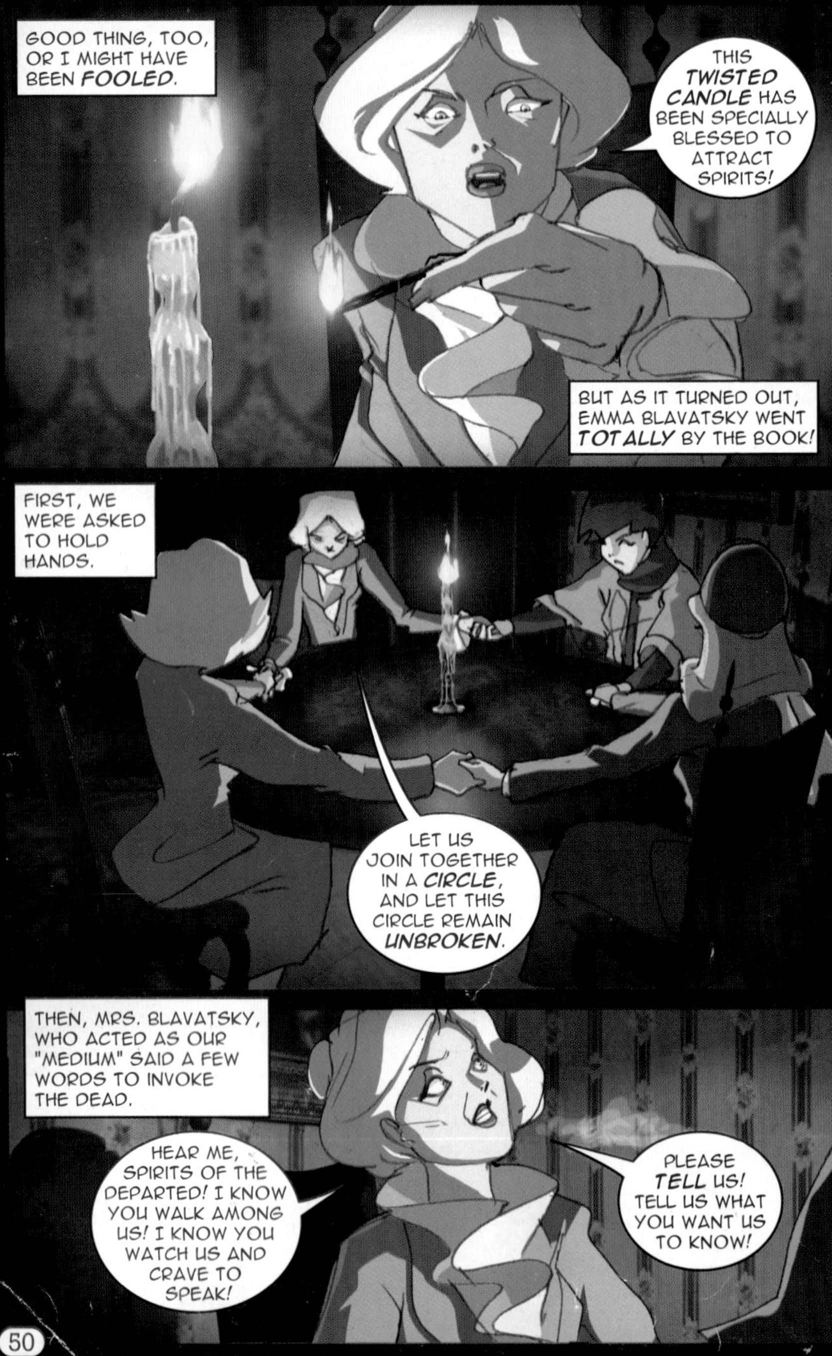
GOOD THING, TOO, OR I MIGHT HAVE BEEN FOOLED.
THIS TWISTED CANDLE HAS BEEN SPECIALLY BLESSED TO ATTRACT SPIRITS!
BUT AS IT TURNED OUT, EMMA BLAVATSKY WENT TOTALLY BY THE BOOK!
FIRST, WE WERE ASKED TO HOLD HANDS.
LET US JOIN TOGETHER IN A CIRCLE, AND LET THIS CIRCLE REMAIN UNBROKEN.
THEN, MRS. BLAVATSKY, WHO ACTED AS OUR "MEDIUM" SAID A FEW WORDS TO INVOKE THE DEAD.
HEAR ME, SPIRITS OF THE DEPARTED! I KNOW YOU WALK AMONG US! I KNOW YOU WATCH US AND CRAVE TO SPEAK!
PLEASE TELL US! TELL US WHAT YOU WANT US TO KNOW!

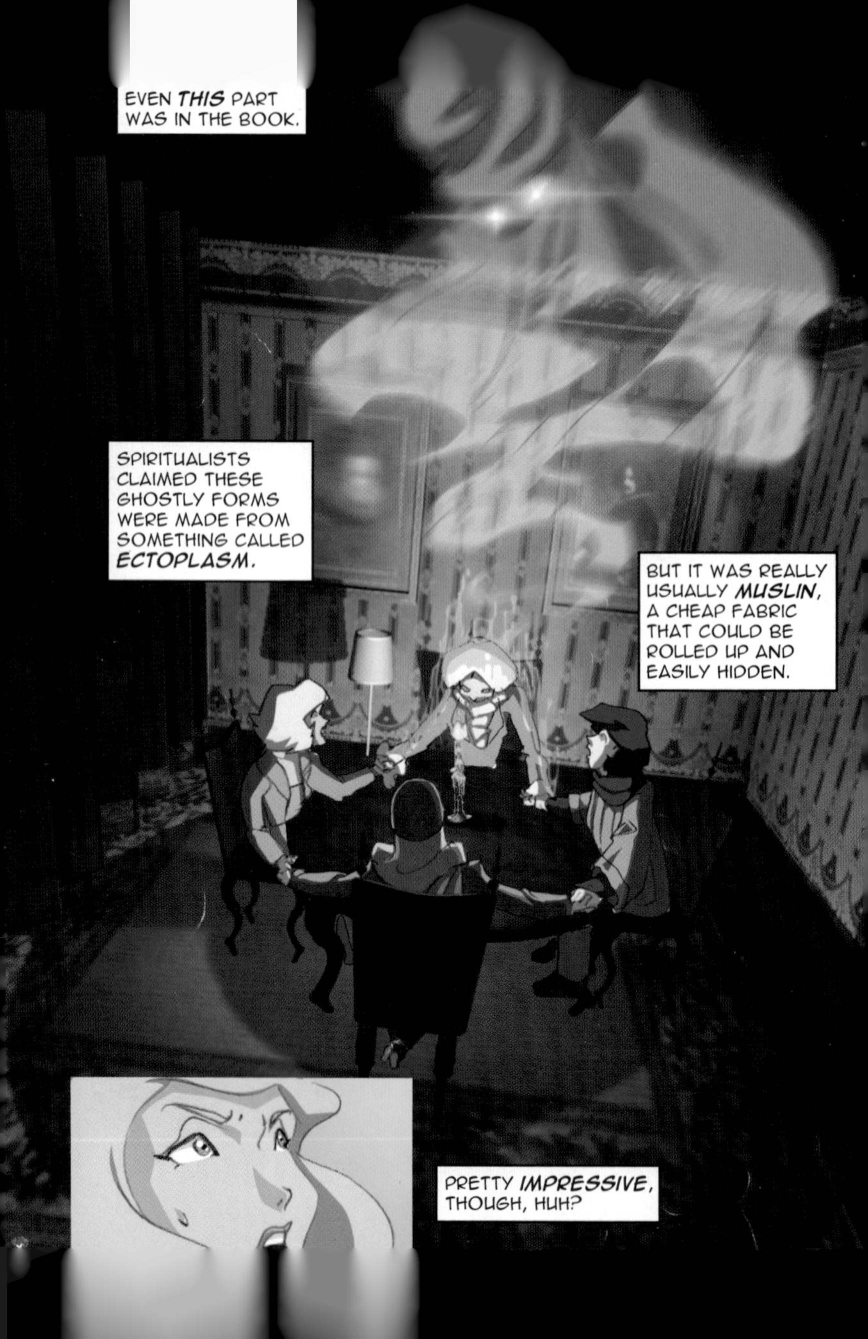
EVEN THIS PART WAS IN THE BOOK.
SPIRITUALISTS CLAIMED THESE GHOSTLY FORMS WERE MADE FROM SOMETHING CALLED ECTOPLASM.
BUT IT WAS REALLY USUALLY MUSLIN, A CHEAP FABRIC THAT COULD BE ROLLED UP AND EASILY HIDDEN.
PRETTY IMPRESSIVE, THOUGH, HUH?

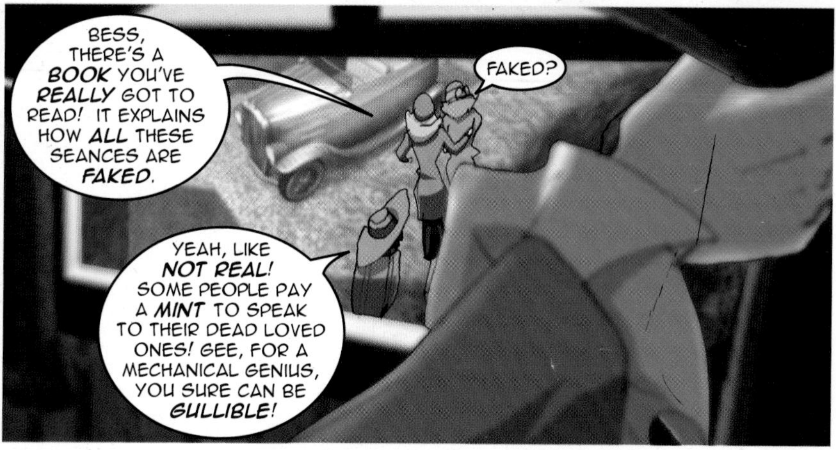
BESS, THERE'S A BOOK YOU'VE REALLY GOT TO READ! IT EXPLAINS HOW ALL THESE SEANCES ARE FAKED.
FAKED?
YEAH, LIKE NOT REAL! SOME PEOPLE PAY A MINT TO SPEAK TO THEIR DEAD LOVED ONES! GEE, FOR A MECHANICAL GENIUS, YOU SURE CAN BE GULLIBLE!

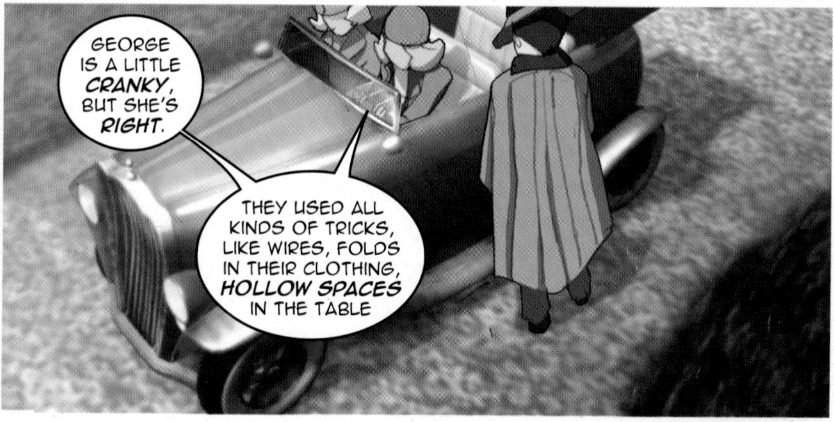
GEORGE IS A LITTLE CRANKY, BUT SHE'S RIGHT.
THEY USED ALL KINDS OF TRICKS, LIKE WIRES, FOLDS IN THEIR CLOTHING, HOLLOW SPACES IN THE TABLE

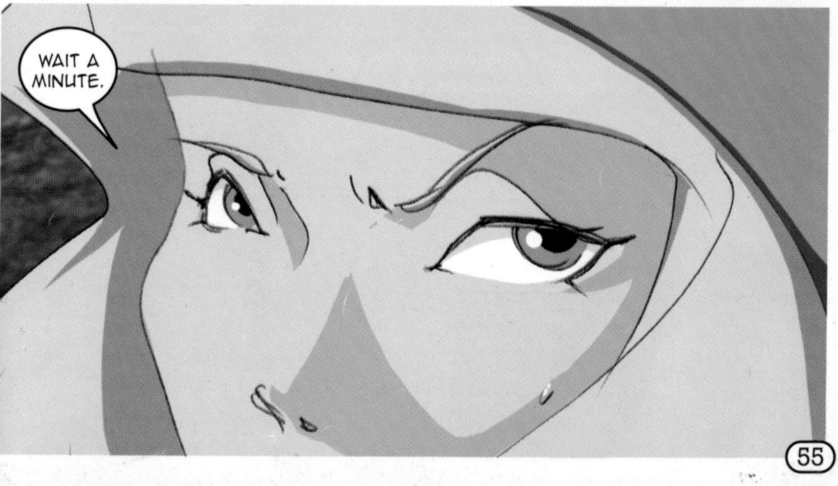
WAIT A MINUTE.

WON'T YOU *PLEASE* LET ME HELP LOOK FOR CLUES, CHIEF McGINNIS?

SORRY, BUT *NO!* CITY HALL IS OFFICIALLY *CLOSED* UNTIL WE GET TO THE BOTTOM OF THIS, AND I PROMISED YOUR FATHER I'D SEND YOU *HOME!*

WHATEVER YOU DO, DO *NOT* HEAD TO LARKSPUR LANE!

THAT PLACE IS FALLING APART! IT'S DANGEROUS WHETHER SOMETHING FISHY IS GOING ON OR *NOT!* LET THE POLICE HANDLE THINGS FOR A CHANGE!

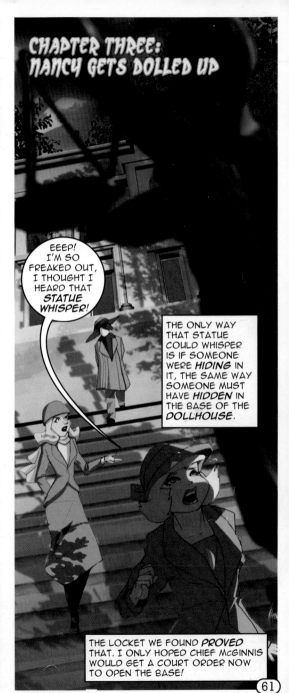

CHAPTER THREE: NANCY GETS DOLLED UP

EEEP! I'M SO FREAKED OUT, I THOUGHT I HEARD THAT *STATUE WHISPER!*

THE ONLY WAY THAT STATUE COULD WHISPER IS IF SOMEONE WERE *HIDING* IN IT, THE SAME WAY SOMEONE MUST HAVE *HIDDEN* IN THE BASE OF THE *DOLLHOUSE*.

THE LOCKET WE FOUND *PROVED* THAT. I ONLY HOPED CHIEF McGINNIS WOULD GET A COURT ORDER NOW TO OPEN THE BASE!

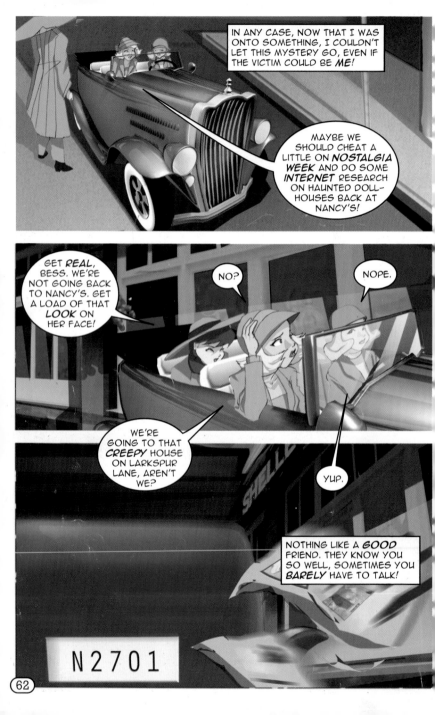

IN ANY CASE, NOW THAT I WAS ONTO SOMETHING, I COULDN'T LET THIS MYSTERY GO, EVEN IF THE VICTIM COULD BE *ME*!

MAYBE WE SHOULD CHEAT A LITTLE ON *NOSTALGIA WEEK* AND DO SOME *INTERNET* RESEARCH ON HAUNTED DOLL-HOUSES BACK AT NANCY'S!

GET *REAL*, BESS. WE'RE NOT GOING BACK TO NANCY'S. GET A LOAD OF THAT *LOOK* ON HER FACE!

NO?

NOPE.

WE'RE GOING TO THAT *CREEPY* HOUSE ON LARKSPUR LANE, AREN'T WE?

YUP.

NOTHING LIKE A *GOOD* FRIEND. THEY KNOW YOU SO WELL, SOMETIMES YOU *BARELY* HAVE TO TALK!

N2701

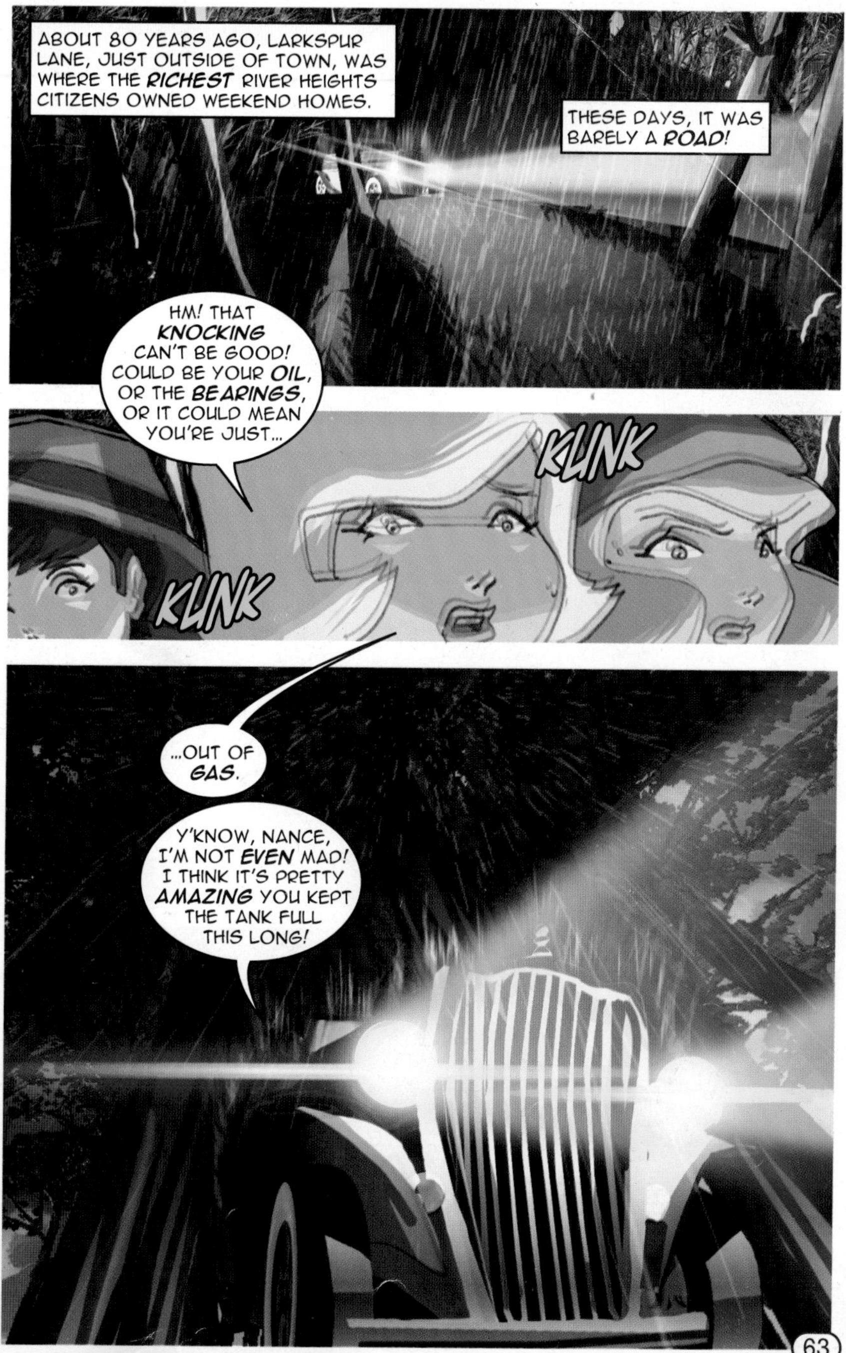

ABOUT 80 YEARS AGO, LARKSPUR LANE, JUST OUTSIDE OF TOWN, WAS WHERE THE RICHEST RIVER HEIGHTS CITIZENS OWNED WEEKEND HOMES.
THESE DAYS, IT WAS BARELY A ROAD!
HM! THAT KNOCKING CAN'T BE GOOD! COULD BE YOUR OIL, OR THE BEARINGS, OR IT COULD MEAN YOU'RE JUST...
KLUNK
KLUNK
...OUT OF GAS.
Y'KNOW, NANCE, I'M NOT EVEN MAD! I THINK IT'S PRETTY AMAZING YOU KEPT THE TANK FULL THIS LONG!

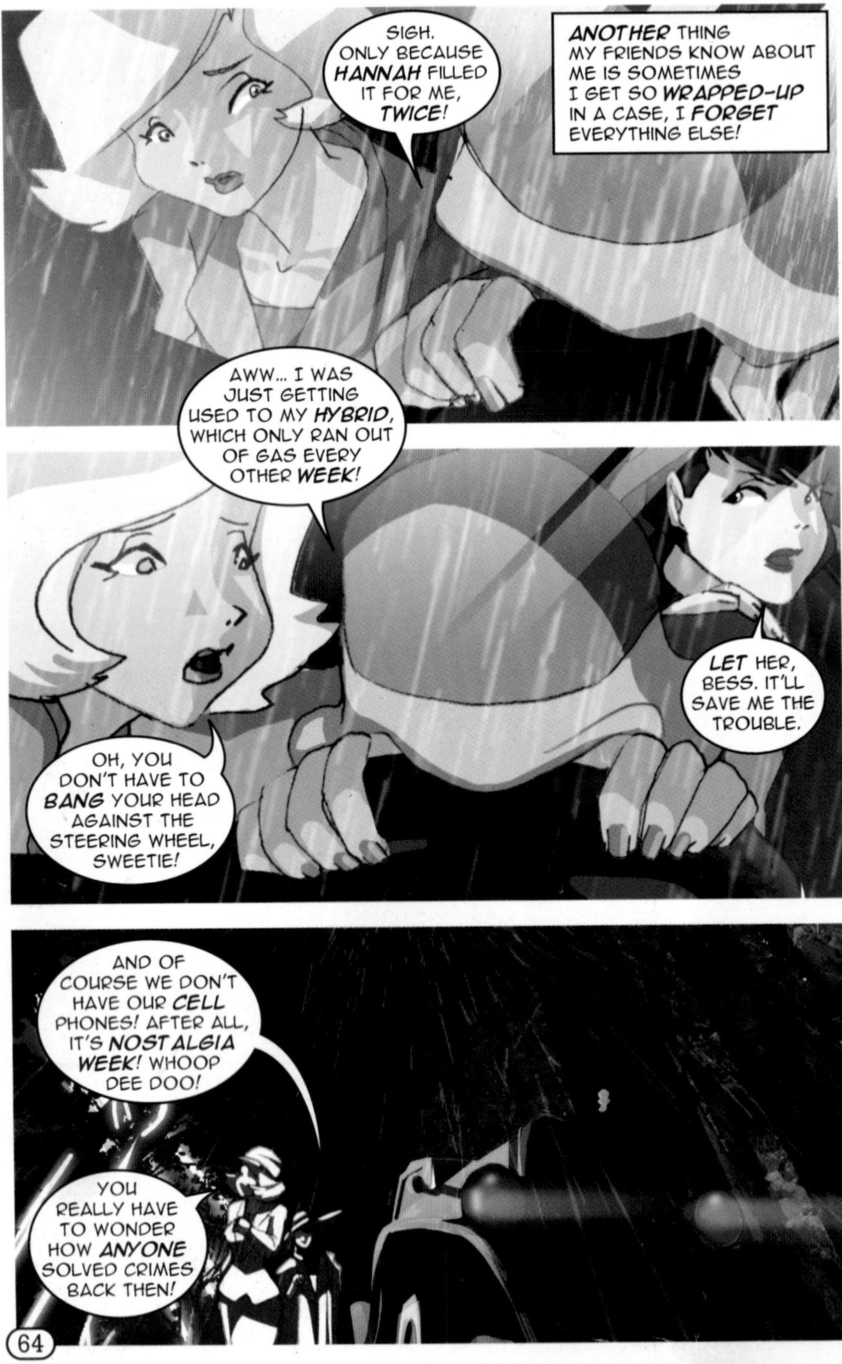
SIGH. ONLY BECAUSE HANNAH FILLED IT FOR ME, TWICE!
ANOTHER THING MY FRIENDS KNOW ABOUT ME IS SOMETIMES I GET SO WRAPPED-UP IN A CASE, I FORGET EVERYTHING ELSE!
AWW... I WAS JUST GETTING USED TO MY HYBRID, WHICH ONLY RAN OUT OF GAS EVERY OTHER WEEK!
LET HER, BESS. IT'LL SAVE ME THE TROUBLE.
OH, YOU DON'T HAVE TO BANG YOUR HEAD AGAINST THE STEERING WHEEL, SWEETIE!
AND OF COURSE WE DON'T HAVE OUR CELL PHONES! AFTER ALL, IT'S NOSTALGIA WEEK! WHOOP DEE DOO!
YOU REALLY HAVE TO WONDER HOW ANYONE SOLVED CRIMES BACK THEN!

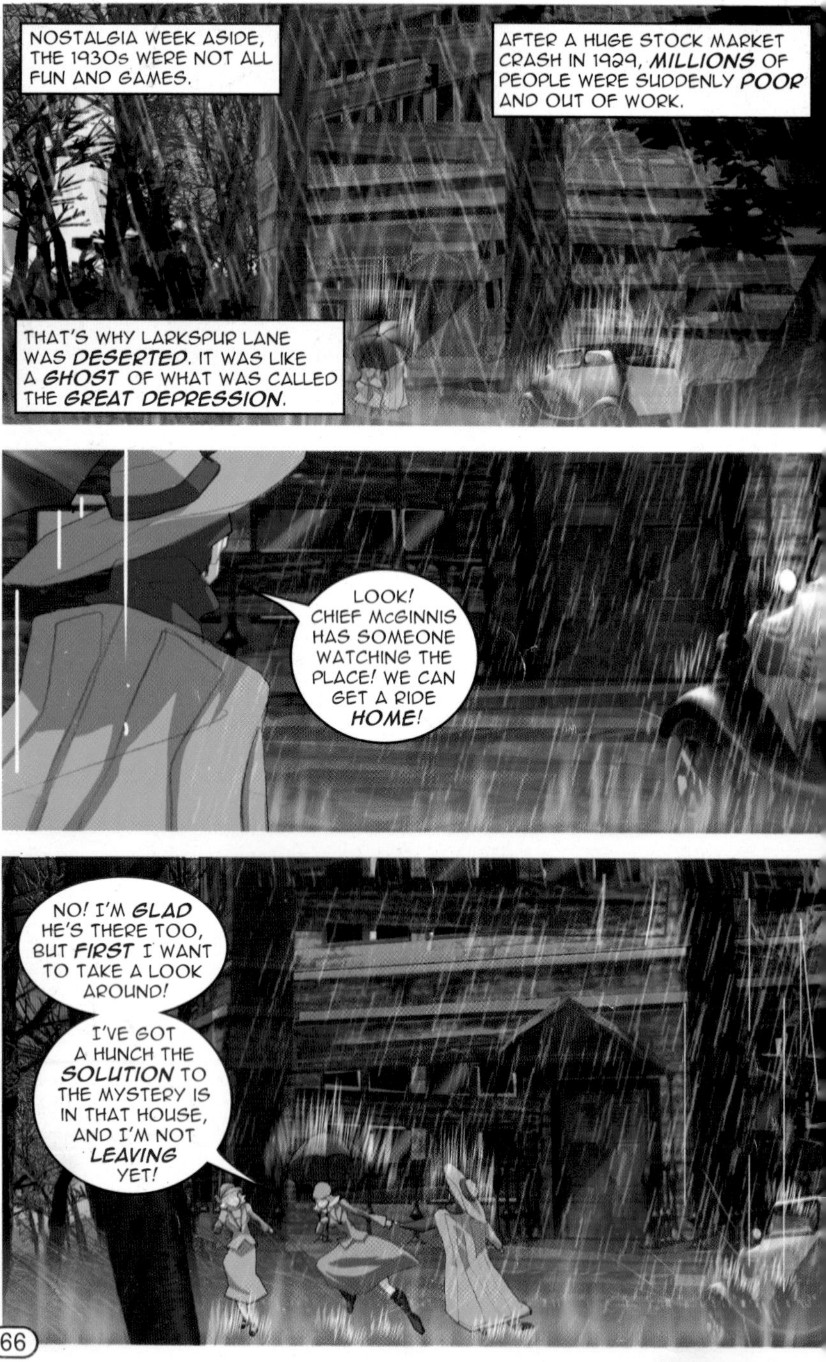
NOSTALGIA WEEK ASIDE, THE 1930s WERE NOT ALL FUN AND GAMES.
AFTER A HUGE STOCK MARKET CRASH IN 1929, MILLIONS OF PEOPLE WERE SUDDENLY POOR AND OUT OF WORK.
THAT'S WHY LARKSPUR LANE WAS DESERTED. IT WAS LIKE A GHOST OF WHAT WAS CALLED THE GREAT DEPRESSION.
LOOK! CHIEF McGINNIS HAS SOMEONE WATCHING THE PLACE! WE CAN GET A RIDE HOME!
NO! I'M GLAD HE'S THERE TOO, BUT FIRST I WANT TO TAKE A LOOK AROUND!
I'VE GOT A HUNCH THE SOLUTION TO THE MYSTERY IS IN THAT HOUSE, AND I'M NOT LEAVING YET!

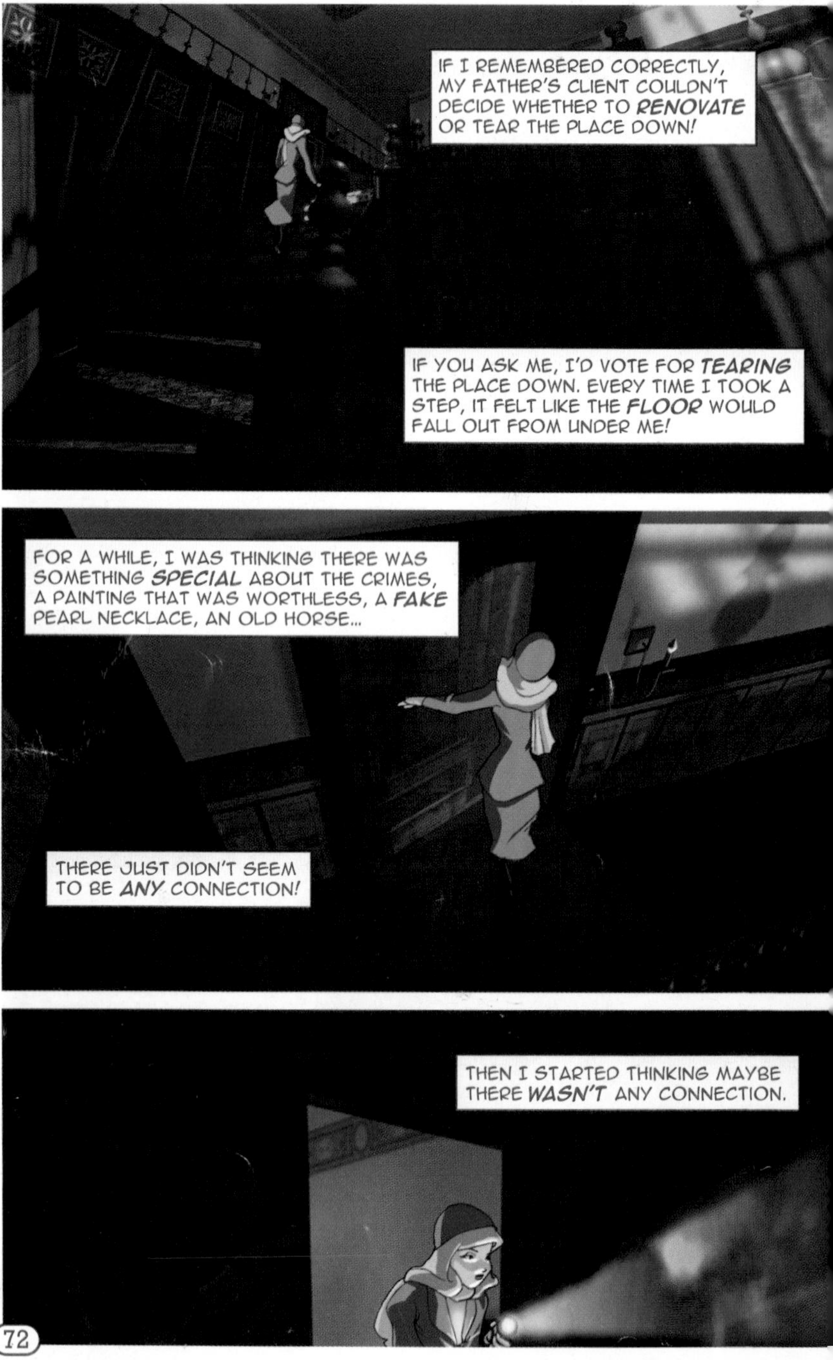
IF I REMEMBERED CORRECTLY, MY FATHER'S CLIENT COULDN'T DECIDE WHETHER TO RENOVATE OR TEAR THE PLACE DOWN!
IF YOU ASK ME, I'D VOTE FOR TEARING THE PLACE DOWN. EVERY TIME I TOOK A STEP, IT FELT LIKE THE FLOOR WOULD FALL OUT FROM UNDER ME!
FOR A WHILE, I WAS THINKING THERE WAS SOMETHING SPECIAL ABOUT THE CRIMES, A PAINTING THAT WAS WORTHLESS, A FAKE PEARL NECKLACE, AN OLD HORSE...
THERE JUST DIDN'T SEEM TO BE ANY CONNECTION!
THEN I STARTED THINKING MAYBE THERE WASN'T ANY CONNECTION.

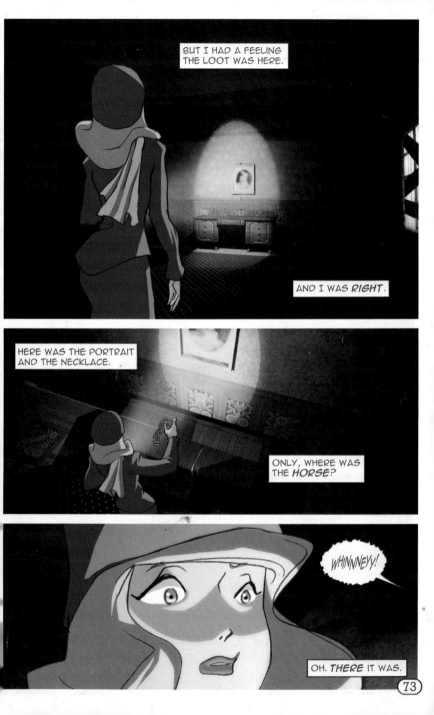

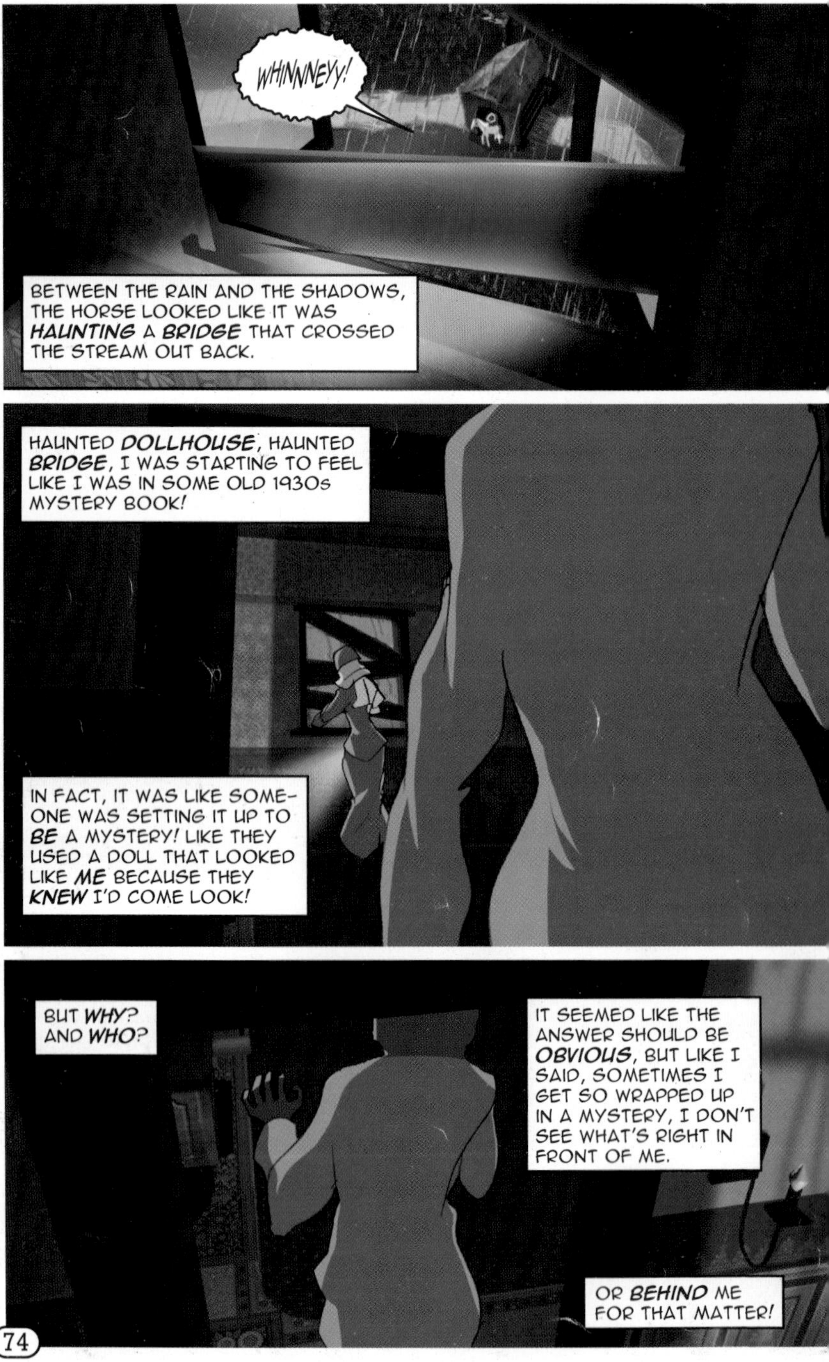
WHINNNEYY!
BETWEEN THE RAIN AND THE SHADOWS, THE HORSE LOOKED LIKE IT WAS HAUNTING A BRIDGE THAT CROSSED THE STREAM OUT BACK.
HAUNTED DOLLHOUSE, HAUNTED BRIDGE, I WAS STARTING TO FEEL LIKE I WAS IN SOME OLD 1930s MYSTERY BOOK!
IN FACT, IT WAS LIKE SOME-ONE WAS SETTING IT UP TO BE A MYSTERY! LIKE THEY USED A DOLL THAT LOOKED LIKE ME BECAUSE THEY KNEW I'D COME LOOK!
BUT WHY? AND WHO?
IT SEEMED LIKE THE ANSWER SHOULD BE OBVIOUS, BUT LIKE I SAID, SOMETIMES I GET SO WRAPPED UP IN A MYSTERY, I DON'T SEE WHAT'S RIGHT IN FRONT OF ME.
OR BEHIND ME FOR THAT MATTER!

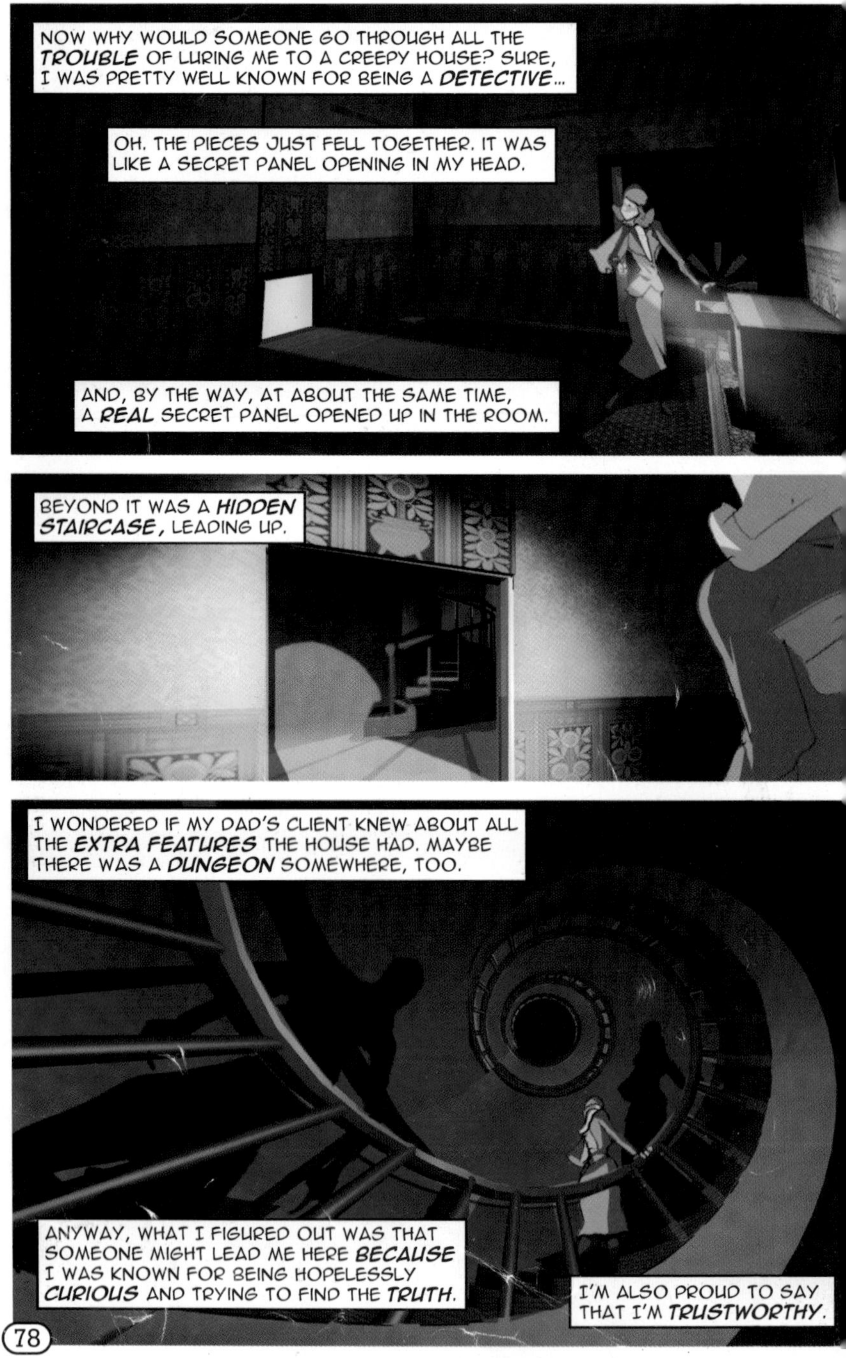
NOW WHY WOULD SOMEONE GO THROUGH ALL THE TROUBLE OF LURING ME TO A CREEPY HOUSE? SURE, I WAS PRETTY WELL KNOWN FOR BEING A DETECTIVE...
OH. THE PIECES JUST FELL TOGETHER. IT WAS LIKE A SECRET PANEL OPENING IN MY HEAD.
AND, BY THE WAY, AT ABOUT THE SAME TIME, A REAL SECRET PANEL OPENED UP IN THE ROOM.
BEYOND IT WAS A HIDDEN STAIRCASE, LEADING UP.
I WONDERED IF MY DAD'S CLIENT KNEW ABOUT ALL THE EXTRA FEATURES THE HOUSE HAD. MAYBE THERE WAS A DUNGEON SOMEWHERE, TOO.
ANYWAY, WHAT I FIGURED OUT WAS THAT SOMEONE MIGHT LEAD ME HERE BECAUSE I WAS KNOWN FOR BEING HOPELESSLY CURIOUS AND TRYING TO FIND THE TRUTH.
I'M ALSO PROUD TO SAY THAT I'M TRUSTWORTHY.

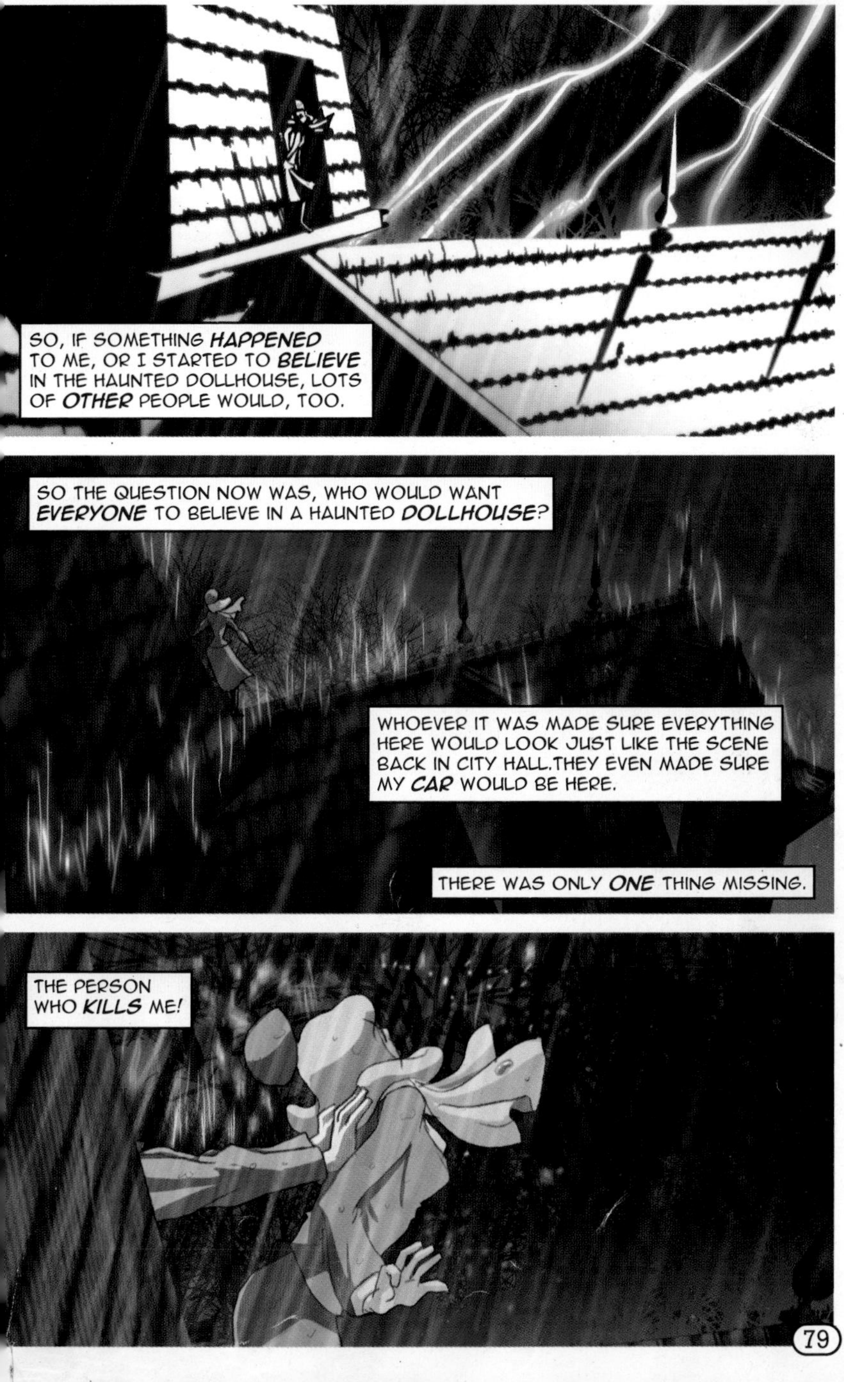
SO, IF SOMETHING HAPPENED TO ME, OR I STARTED TO BELIEVE IN THE HAUNTED DOLLHOUSE, LOTS OF OTHER PEOPLE WOULD, TOO.
SO THE QUESTION NOW WAS, WHO WOULD WANT EVERYONE TO BELIEVE IN A HAUNTED DOLLHOUSE?
WHOEVER IT WAS MADE SURE EVERYTHING HERE WOULD LOOK JUST LIKE THE SCENE BACK IN CITY HALL. THEY EVEN MADE SURE MY CAR WOULD BE HERE.
THERE WAS ONLY ONE THING MISSING.
THE PERSON WHO KILLS ME!

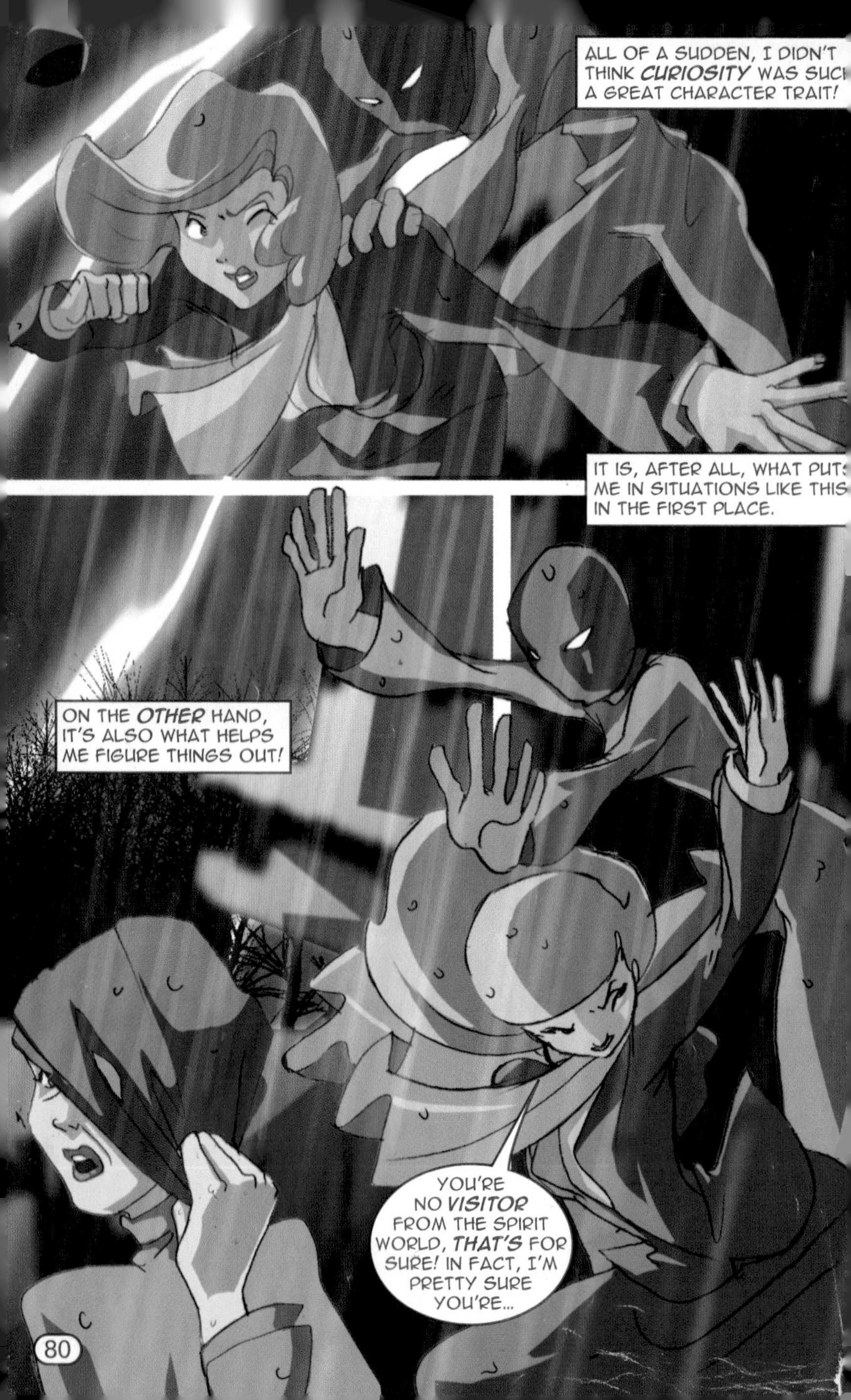
ALL OF A SUDDEN, I DIDN'T THINK *CURIOSITY* WAS SUC
A GREAT CHARACTER TRAIT!
IT IS, AFTER ALL, WHAT PUT
ME IN SITUATIONS LIKE THIS IN THE FIRST PLACE.
ON THE *OTHER* HAND, IT'S ALSO WHAT HELPS ME FIGURE THINGS OUT!
YOU'RE NO *VISITOR* FROM THE SPIRIT WORLD, *THAT'S* FOR SURE! IN FACT, I'M PRETTY SURE YOU'RE...

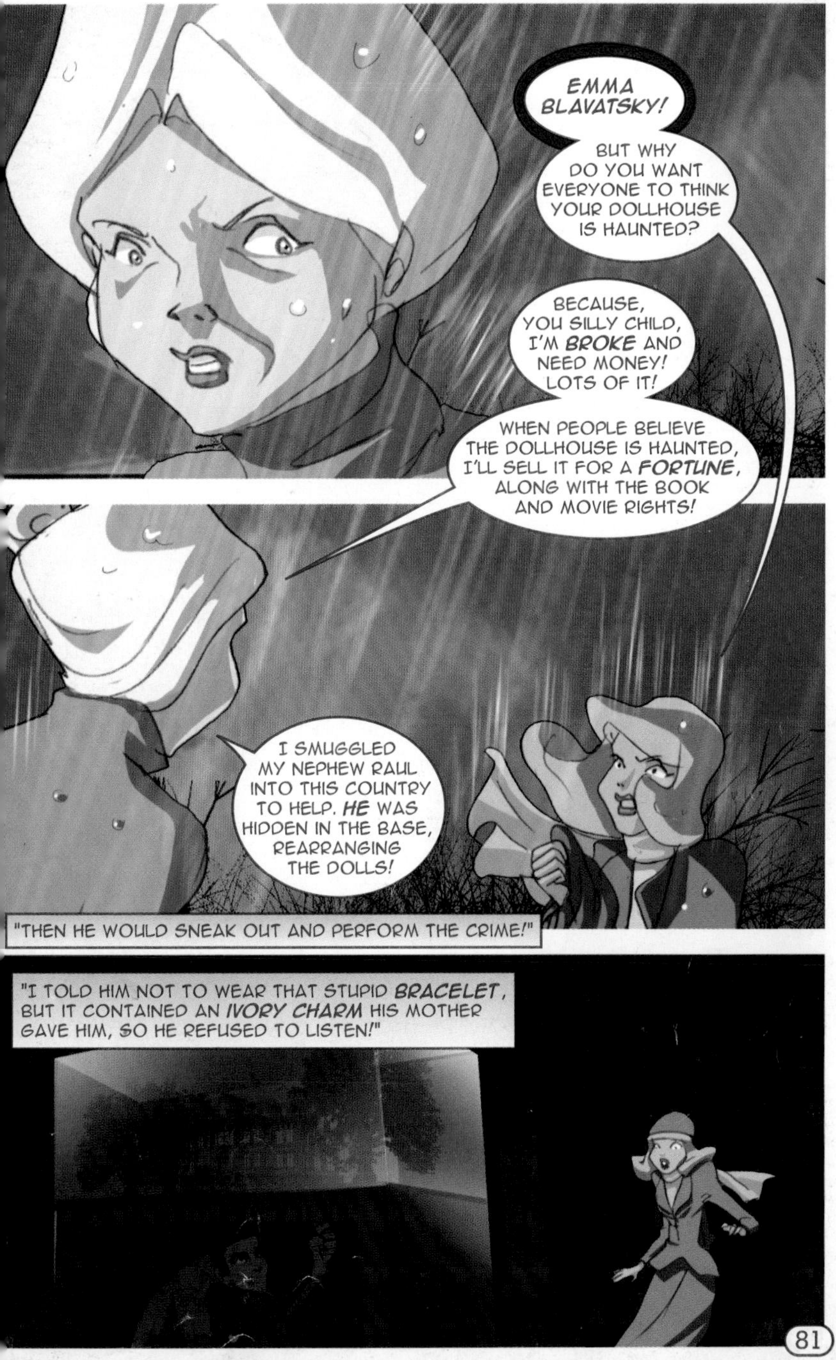
EMMA BLAVATSKY!
BUT WHY DO YOU WANT EVERYONE TO THINK YOUR DOLLHOUSE IS HAUNTED?
BECAUSE, YOU SILLY CHILD, I'M **BROKE** AND NEED MONEY! LOTS OF IT!
WHEN PEOPLE BELIEVE THE DOLLHOUSE IS HAUNTED, I'LL SELL IT FOR A **FORTUNE**, ALONG WITH THE BOOK AND MOVIE RIGHTS!
I SMUGGLED MY NEPHEW RAUL INTO THIS COUNTRY TO HELP. **HE** WAS HIDDEN IN THE BASE, REARRANGING THE DOLLS!
"THEN HE WOULD SNEAK OUT AND PERFORM THE CRIME!"
"I TOLD HIM NOT TO WEAR THAT STUPID **BRACELET**, BUT IT CONTAINED AN **IVORY CHARM** HIS MOTHER GAVE HIM, SO HE REFUSED TO LISTEN!"

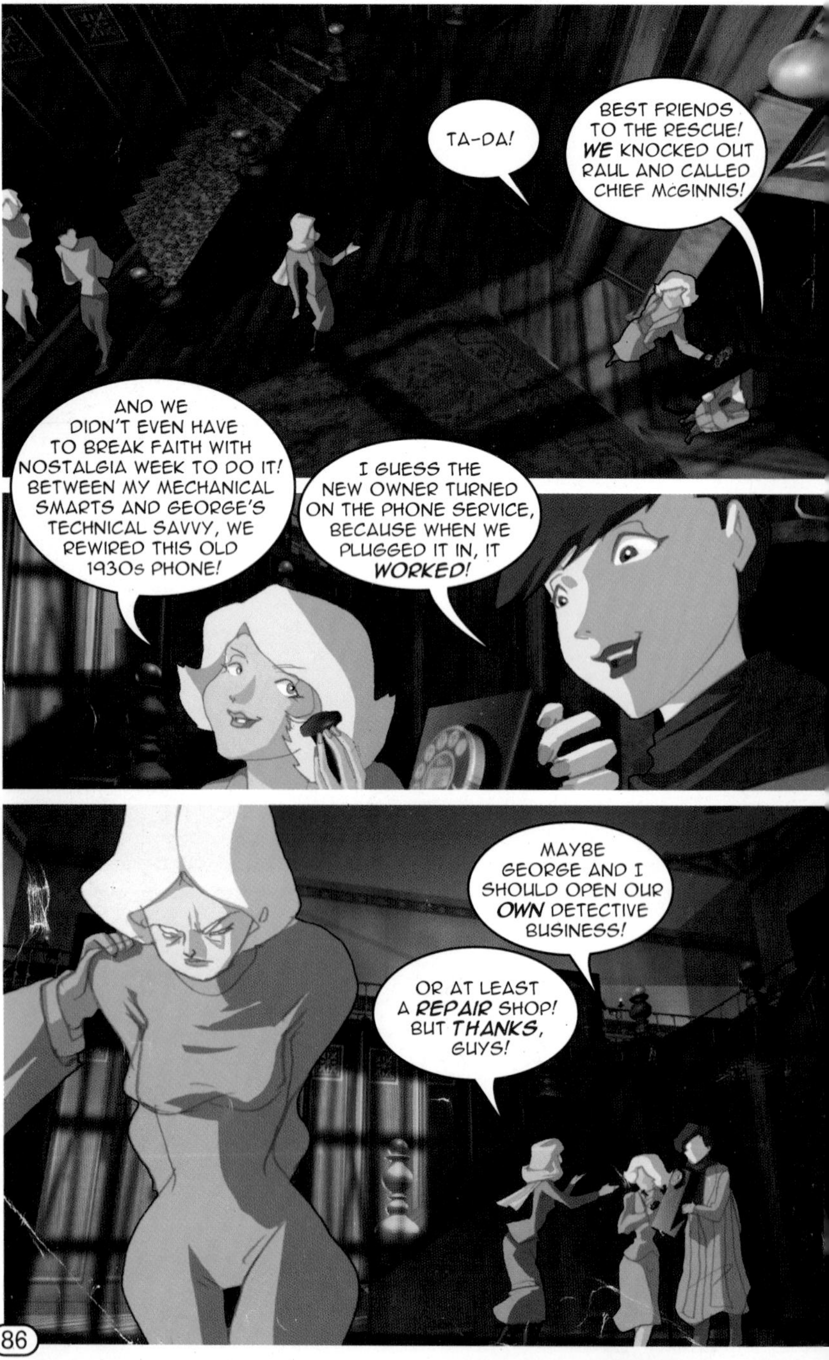
TA-DA!
BEST FRIENDS TO THE RESCUE! WE KNOCKED OUT RAUL AND CALLED CHIEF McGINNIS!
AND WE DIDN'T EVEN HAVE TO BREAK FAITH WITH NOSTALGIA WEEK TO DO IT! BETWEEN MY MECHANICAL SMARTS AND GEORGE'S TECHNICAL SAVVY, WE REWIRED THIS OLD 1930s PHONE!
I GUESS THE NEW OWNER TURNED ON THE PHONE SERVICE, BECAUSE WHEN WE PLUGGED IT IN, IT WORKED!
MAYBE GEORGE AND I SHOULD OPEN OUR OWN DETECTIVE BUSINESS!
OR AT LEAST A REPAIR SHOP! BUT THANKS, GUYS!

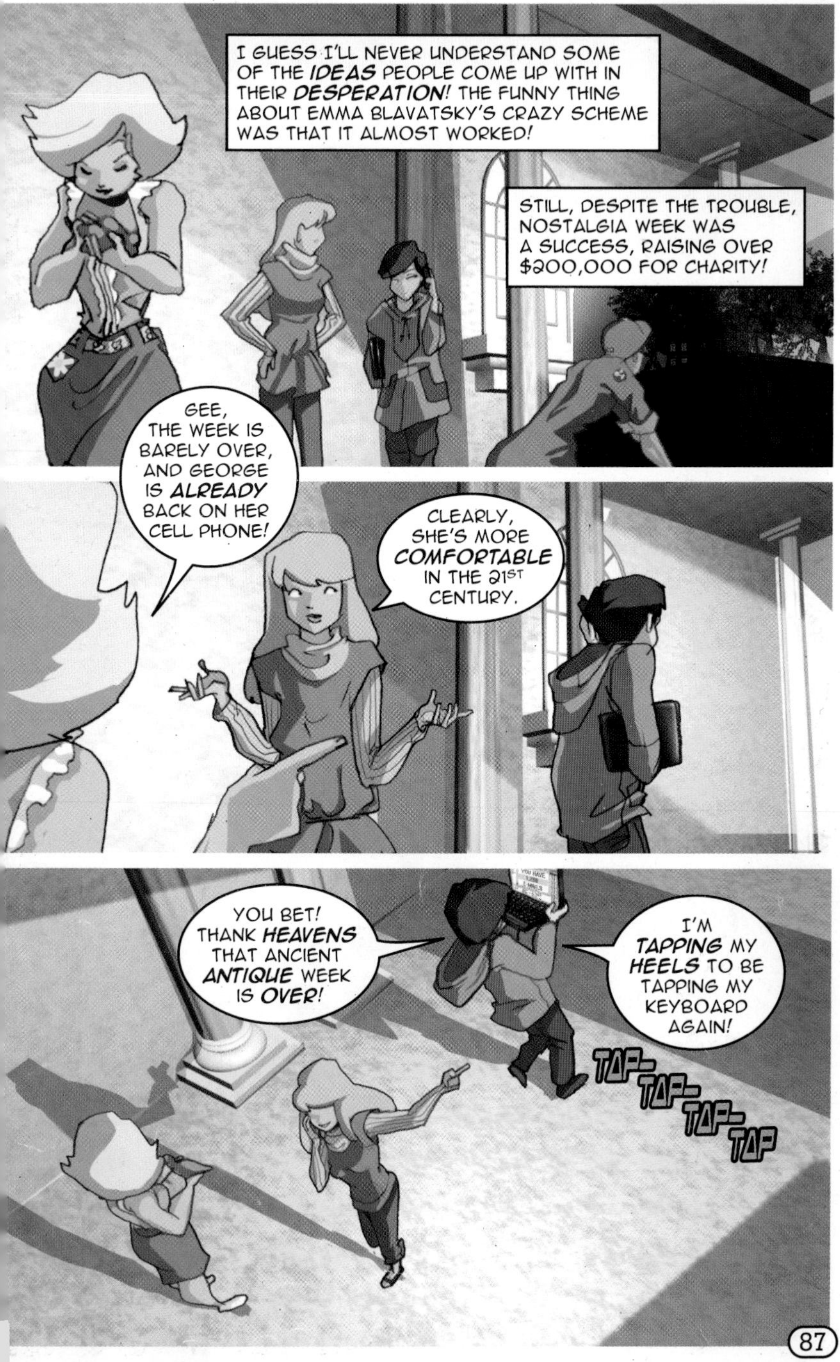
I GUESS I'LL NEVER UNDERSTAND SOME OF THE IDEAS PEOPLE COME UP WITH IN THEIR DESPERATION! THE FUNNY THING ABOUT EMMA BLAVATSKY'S CRAZY SCHEME WAS THAT IT ALMOST WORKED!
STILL, DESPITE THE TROUBLE, NOSTALGIA WEEK WAS A SUCCESS, RAISING OVER $200,000 FOR CHARITY!
GEE, THE WEEK IS BARELY OVER, AND GEORGE IS ALREADY BACK ON HER CELL PHONE!
CLEARLY, SHE'S MORE COMFORTABLE IN THE 21ST CENTURY.
YOU BET! THANK HEAVENS THAT ANCIENT ANTIQUE WEEK IS OVER!
I'M TAPPING MY HEELS TO BE TAPPING MY KEYBOARD AGAIN!
TAP-TAP-TAP-TAP